To:
Erin
Thanks for your
support!

LARONYA

TEAGUE

Social Work: The Carolyn Black Chronicles

Dear God I thank you and I will never let go of your hand...

Laronya Teague

"The Lord is my light and my salvation; WHOM SHALL I FEAR"
Psalms 27

"Yea, though I walk through the valley of the shadow of death, I will fear no evil; for thou art with me; Thy Rod and Thy Staff, they comfort me" –Psalms 23:4

"God has not given us a spirit of fear, but of power, love and of a sound mind"
2 Timothy 1:7

"What is one thing you would do if you knew you would not fail? Now go out and do it"-Sam From the movie *New Year's Eve*

Dedication

This book is dedicated to all the Social Workers, Therapists, Psychologists, Foster Care Workers, Psychiatrists, Mental Health Technicians, Qualified Professionals, Associate Professionals and Residential Care Specialists that devote their time, effort and energy
to protecting children,
inspiring the uninspired,
giving hope to the hopeless,
creating another perspective for those who can't see beyond what's in front of them
and providing people with the opportunity to having a better quality of life.
Don't be deterred by the red tape because if one child is safe, one family is reunited, one teenager is inspired and one person recovers their lost smile then your blood, sweat and tears are not in vain.

Last but definitely not least, where would I be without my inspirations, my embers; Sharika, Crystal and Shektia. Thanks for always believing in me and encouraging me to pick up my pen again.
I love you all dearly and this book is dedicated to you…I hope you enjoy reading it as much as I've enjoyed writing it.

Prologue

Introducing Carolyn Black

Hello, my name is Carolyn Black. I am a Child Protective Services (CPS) Investigator for the Fosterberg County Department of Social Services. I investigate CPS reports to determine the validity and severity of abuse or neglect inflicted on children under the age of 18. If reports of abuse or neglect are determined valid, then the CPS team meets and discusses the necessary actions that need to be taken. My team is composed of myself and four other CPS workers: Valerie Whitman; who is my supervisor, Mario Scott, Jenetta Bryant and Zian Williams. We all carry our own caseload but work together when handling difficult situations. And based off the severity of the circumstances, some children have to be removed from their homes immediately. In these instances, parents can be very hostile and irrational therefore requiring us to approach the situation in pairs or with a police escort. For the most part, I personally don't need any help because I know how to interact with people and I'm straight up with them. I don't go into their homes with an authoritarian attitude as if I'm better than them. I let them know why I'm there and what they can do to avoid relinquishing their parental rights. But in the event that the "professional approach" doesn't work; I carry a switchblade in my bra, I'm a kick boxer and my dad taught me how to street fight. Some people say I'm cocky but I say I'm confident. I was bullied *a lot* throughout my adolescent and early teenage years so I had no choice but to learn to fight back. My dad always taught me to be cautious in potentially hostile situations but he compelled me to be able to protect myself. And I don't discriminate when it comes to these families and anybody else for that matter. I do everything I can to remain professional, empathetic and just. But if I ever feel threatened then I resort to survival mode and its either going to be me or them. My supervisor calls me hotheaded and says that I overstep my boundaries sometimes but I if I have to get a little rough to protect these children or myself then so be it.

My coworkers and I work together well for the most part but we are a diverse group with very different personalities. Sometimes those personalities don't mesh which causes personal conflicts; however we never allow those things to affect our jobs. Zian is the youngest on the team. She's very friendly and pleasant but she's too apprehensive and timid. I understand that she's young and wet behind the ears in this profession so I try to teach her things; but most of the time she just doesn't get it. Jenetta is a backstabbing heifer who is so mercurial that *she* doesn't know if she's coming or going. She's a liar who doesn't have a shred of loyalty and only a morsel of integrity. I can't stand her and I'm sure that the feeling is mutual but we deal with each other because of our job. Mario on the other hand is my buddy. We've known each other for a while and we get along very well. He makes me laugh and we always sit together at staff meetings or any other function so we can giggle and joke on Jenetta. She's in love with Mario but he dislikes her just about as much as I do. He knows how malicious she is just like everyone else. Valerie; our supervisor, is the peacemaker and tries to keep us all from killing each other. She does a fairly good job at it because she's very assertive and doesn't mind telling us "I love you but I will definitely fire you." She doesn't allow petty things to go on and demands that we keep any personal drama at home. As long as we do our jobs and do them efficiently, she could care less about what goes on outside of that.

I take my job very seriously and I am very good at what I do. I work long hard hours, but it pays off because at the end of the day, I know that I have done something to help keep a child healthy and safe. Sometimes my job is very frustrating and difficult but I get a lot of pleasure from my career and I look forward to going to work mostly every day. My job is very stressful so when work is over, I like to indulge in any stress reliever that I deem effective at that time. My favorite and most frequently used form of stress relief is marijuana. It relaxes me, it soothes me and it induces my desire to play with my toys; my toys being men. I indulge in a delectable selection of men and they all serve a different purpose and fulfill a different need or desire. By doing this, I have enabled myself to keep from having to deal with the ups and downs and roller coasters that are associated with long term, committed relationships. I merely pick a "toy" off the shelf and when I get bored with playing with him, I put him back on the shelf and retrieve a different toy.

I'm a beautiful, smart and grounded woman but I have learned that those things do not make one immune to cheating, beating and being used. I have been hurt so many times that I'm numb. Growing up being fair skinned was a double edged sword for me because the girls hated me and the boys only wanted to sleep with me. I admit that I was one of the prettiest girls in school and my head got big. I was blinded by all the attention and thought it was cool to sleep around because "everybody wanted me." I didn't realize until it was too late that I was just another notch or the subject of a bet. Once I caught on, no one wanted me because they no longer had to work for me. I was viewed as being easy and no longer as a challenge. So I began getting into unhealthy and unfulfilling relationships whereby I did everything to make things work, only to end up with a broken spirit and a broken heart. I went through a lot but as a result I now know all the tricks of the trade. I no longer give my Juicy away only to get nothing in return. I no longer deal with a man who can't bring anything to the table. I no longer commit myself to one man when I can have several different ones that I can simultaneously take a piece of and create the "whole man" that I so desire. And since I chose to exclusively date married men, I don't have to be in a forced commitment. All the cards are on the table so there are no surprises. I have no desire to be with these men beyond what they can do for me therefore I don't have to worry about getting hurt. Plus there are a lot of other perks that come with dating married men. They want a side chick to fulfill their sexual desires and fantasies and I simply thrive off the fact that I get a different sexual experience each and every time. They want to please me just as much as I want to please them. They want to keep me happy and although I'm aware that it's superficial, it works and eliminates stress. I call when I want to, I only meet when I want to and I definitely only have sex when I want to. All the while, I still get expensive gifts, extravagant trips and I have a nice size bank account.

Dewayne is an older man who is very dapper with very exquisite taste. He's warm and friendly and I really enjoy his company. He's a very successful heart surgeon and he keeps me draped in fine clothes and jewelry. He even paid my whole way through grad school. He likes being in the company of a beautiful young woman because, I guess, it boosts his ego and makes him feel young. He's very attentive and affectionate. He's quaint and charming and he makes me feel beautiful and dainty. And although Dewayne has a small penis he realizes it and therefore accommodates me by exquisitely taking care my Juicy with his tongue until she melts all over his face. When I'm with him, he and I reside in our world of refined and elegant bliss. He takes me to balls and operas or plays. When we make love he takes his time with me and I in return whisper whatever he wants to hear in his ear. We usually meet monthly because his wife is a bicoastal manager for some hot shot company and she is gone at least one week out of the month. Next on the toy list is Brad. He's a filthy rich architect who just happens to be white. He takes me with him around the world because he likes the way I look and he likes to show me off. Upon first glance, most people can't pinpoint what race I am. I get all kinds of labels ranging from Hispanic to Middle Easterner. I'm five foot four, with long dark brown hair that I can rock curly or straight. I have sandy brown skin, dark brown eyes, pouty lips and an hour glass figure that would make video vixens insecure. Brad loves it because he's a very vain person and his wife; poor thing, has had four children and with the kids went her body and her self esteem. She used to be gorgeous but, after the kids she allowed herself to go down. Brad; being the narcissistic man that he is, would not dare have his overseas business partners see him with a woman of her defeated caliber. They all probably think that I'm his wife because I travel with him more than she does. I know I'm Brad's trophy chick but I really don't care because he makes me feel powerful and exotic and I can be just as narcissistic as he is. He keeps my account full and takes me to the most extraordinary places the world has to offer. He's fulfilled my dream of seeing many of the Wonders of the World and for that, I'm greatly appreciative. His sex is awesome and very spontaneous. He's wild and carefree in bed but he's very cocky otherwise. Sometimes our strong personalities collide and we end up having intense disagreements but the sex that follows is also intense and explosive. Brad and I only see each other sporadically because our work schedules are so different but he calls at least once a week and we try to take short weekend trips as often as possible.

Then there's Jermaine. There's not too much to say about Jermaine with the exception that he's dumb as a box of rocks but he's fine and bangs like a porno star. Jermaine is nothing but a booty call that I contact when I'm horny and none of my other "toys" are available. Jermaine is probably the best in bed because he's kinky and I'm a freak. Jermaine fulfills my needs by tapping into my Juicy's deepest, darkest fantasies and desires. I call Jermaine every once in a while to break me off, then I send his ass home. I really don't know too much about him. I met him at a Coffee Shop while I was at a conference in Boone, NC. I know that he's not married but he's in a relationship with some girl from his home town. He is very cautious about using protection (as am I) and goes to the clinic regularly. When he and I meet it's usually at a nice hotel in Boone. We do our thing and go our separate ways. There is usually very little conversation and he always pays for the room.

Last but most definitely not least, is Demarcus. Out of all the men on my "toy list", he means the most to me. He's not rich but he makes me laugh and I always feel so desired and special around him. He's great in bed and we always have such engaging, interesting conversations. I can let my hair down and be myself with him. He's one of the few people I trust to engage in my favorite habit of smoking marijuana with. He's just all around fun to be with. He's like a breath of fresh air; a relief from stress. I've known him for years and we've always had an on again, off again, relationship. We started dating my junior year in undergrad and continued dealing with each other until about 3 years ago when he told me that he had gotten a girl pregnant and was planning to marry her. I was devastated but I charged it to the game because although we cared a lot for each other we had never taken our relationship to a committed level. We got along well but we have always been at two different places in our lives which limited us to a friend with benefits relationship. But nevertheless; although we both saw other people and would be separated for long periods of time, we always seemed to find our way back to each other.

We recently reconnected and it was like we picked right up from where we left off. I know that he's married, but I doubt that we will ever leave each other alone. Not to mention, his wife is the poster child for a hood rat. Demarcus would have never married her if he wouldn't have gotten her pregnant. It was the quintessential story of guy goes to the club, has too much to drink, preys in on an easy "kill" for the night, has a one night stand, gets her pregnant and is then stuck. He's told me about how much he despises his wife but he is adamant about raising his son in a two parent home since he grew up in the foster care system. And although his wife has fire engine red hair with five different hair styles woven into one and five different personalities to match; he stays because he really loves his son. Demarcus comes to me for good meals, meaningful conversation and peace. I am his escape from reality and he is mine. I go to him for solace, familiarity and intimacy. And for that reason he is dangerous for me because he's pushes me to where I almost compromise my established unbreakable rule about the men I deal with: get my needs fulfilled and refrain from letting my emotions get involved. Because of our history and deep bond I've allowed him to cross a boundary that none of the others have been privy to cross. He makes me *feel.* I try to stay away from Demarcus but the way he makes me feel is addictive and it seduces me to want him as often as I can get him. The good thing is that I really only see Demarcus maybe once every two or three months; mainly when his hood rat wife is in jail or visiting family. I will cancel any trip or obligation that I have for Demarcus because I know our time is precious and limited. I try to restrain myself and be tough but our connection is so strong that it would be like fighting a losing battle.

My friends and family are unaware of my extracurricular activities and I'm going to make sure that it stays that way. My parents are very religious and were adamant about instilling Christ in my life. And although I could be a very spiritual woman, my pride and shame of the things I do before God keeps me from having the relationship that I used to have with Him. I'm afraid to talk to Him because I know that He is not pleased with the way I am living my life. I realize how hypocritical my actions are; therefore I hide from Him and continue going through the motions.

My parents and I are very close. I talk to my mom everyday but I keep our conversations very generic and basic. My mom would die and my dad would kick my ass if they knew that I was sleeping around with married men. They have been together for thirty five years and I have never known them to fight, cheat or hurt each other. Yes they had their disagreements but they always managed to work things out. They still act as if they are just as in love now as they were when I was a small child. They have set the bar high and are great role models in regards to the way a relationship should be. For this reason I just don't understand why my relationships are so contrary to what I have seen and know is right.

I have three siblings: two sisters and one brother and although I have the most education and an established career; I feel like the black sheep out of the family. My sisters and I don't get along and we rarely speak to each other. I am the youngest girl and the only one with a fair complexion. They both have my dad's dark Dominican and Black complexion and I get mine from my mom who is of Cherokee, Irish and Black decent. We all have been blessed with curvy bodies and beautiful faces, but nevertheless the "color" line has always seemed to divide us. Growing up, my sisters acted as if they hated me and they rarely included me in the things that they did. My parents tried hard to bridge the gap between us but nothing ever seemed to work. As I've gotten older, I've learned to accept their discontentment but I definitely don't take their crap anymore. Family events are always tense because they always seem to find a way to patronize me. They come with their husbands and children and because I'm alone they try to make me feel worthless.

My brother and I, on the other hand, are extremely close. He's a year younger than me and being that he's a boy I assume that there is no need for competition. I know that he feels like he's always in the middle of the mess going on between me and my sisters because he has a great relationship with all of us. They recognize that we are closer because he and I are a year apart. As a result, when we're all together, they try to block any interactions between him and me. Then I end up sitting alone or clinging to my parents. They are convinced that I am my parent's favorite and although that might be true, I'd much rather hang out with my siblings than my parents. I tried talking to them, I tried sucking up to them but none of those things worked. Eventually I gave up and stopped going around my family when my sisters were around. I only stop by to see my parents when I know they're alone or on holidays when I don't have a choice.

Female friends are nonexistent in my life. Most females; especially those with boyfriends or husbands, don't want to associate themselves with me because they are intimidated. After getting into so many fights and getting my feelings hurt when I was younger, I tried to cover up my body and make myself as unattractive as possible. When I realized that I didn't have to compromise myself for anyone, I gave up on having girlfriends as well. When I was in college I met a girl who I thought that I could form a long lasting friendship with. She was just as beautiful as I was therefore I just knew that things were going to work out. That is until her boyfriend tried to get me to sleep with him. I thought that if I told her immediately then we could resolve the issue. But it backfired because she didn't believe me and thought that it was I who had made advances towards him. I was heartbroken when our friendship ended because I really cared about her and thought that she was a good friend. After that, I just stayed to myself and have remained the Lone Ranger. I get very lonely sometimes because I really don't have anyone to share my deepest, darkest secrets with. But, in actuality, it's ok because with the shit that I've got going on I can't risk anybody knowing anyway. If my secret life were to get out, I would be ruined and my life, as I know it now, would be over.

The only person I do confide in about my life is my supervisor Valerie. We've known each other for years because we both started out working together at DSS. We also went to the same grad school and she's so confident in herself that she's intimidated by no one. She's the closest thing I have to a real friend because she keeps my secrets and doesn't judge me. We don't really hang out or socialize because our relationship is more professional. She's more like my therapist because when I go into her office and close that door, I know that everything I say to her is confidential. She never tries to make me feel like a subordinate although she does a good job of running the show. She always has an open door policy and although she keeps it real with me, she never disregards my feelings.

My job is my sanctuary because it keeps me sane and diverts my attention away from my personal problems. I don't run from them because they are a part of who I am. But sometimes I just need a break. So whereas most people hate going to work, there are times when I hate going home. Sometimes I laugh to myself when I think about my job title; *Social Worker*, because it is so interchangeable within my life. Not only does it apply to my profession but my personal life as well because both are complicated, demanding and for the most part; fulfilling to a certain extent. These are some of the stories of my social life, work and play.

Case #32481: Mommy Dearest

Henry, please don't leave me. Please don't leave, Henry. I'm so sorry. I didn't know! Pleeeease don't leave!" Dora begged as the pitch of her voice inclined to a shrieking level of desperation. She lunged at Henry in an attempt to wrestle him down to the ground but missed him and landed on the floor with a thud. She quickly regrouped as she watched her beloved Henry stomping towards the door with a fierce look of determination and irrevocability. Realizing that he was serious and could not be deterred, she grabbed onto his leg and held onto it as if her life depended on it. In her mind, her life did depend on it because she knew that if she let him go then she would never see him again.

"Get your damn hands off of me, Dora. NOW!" Henry barked, unmoved by her pleas.

"No Henry. Please. You can't leave me. Please don't go!" Dora screamed as she tightened her grip on his leg. He impetuously pushed her head back with the palm of his hand and forcefully kicked his leg to free himself of Dora's grip. But Dora held onto him with every ounce of strength that she possessed. She loved Henry because he was the only man who'd ever truly been good to her and her twin sons. She'd let him move in with her after only knowing him for a short amount of time. He had had no idea about Dora's past and the fact that she was beyond what was considered to be promiscuous. And he definitely didn't look at her like the true trash that she was. He'd genuinely liked Dora and because he didn't have kids of his own, he'd adored her boys. But just like the many other men that had been in and out of Dora's life, he couldn't deal with her crazy mood swings. He'd tried though because she'd told him about her abusive parents and crappy upbringing. He thought that her erratic mood swings were the result her inability to cope with things due to her past. But as time progressed, her behaviors became more and more severe to the point that she'd physically attacked him. The final straw, however, came when he woke up one morning to find that he had sores all around his mouth and penis. And although he was enraged, Henry wasn't the kind of man that beat on women so instead of choking the life out of her like he'd wanted to, he packed his bags.

Once Dora saw that he was leaving her mind flashed back to all the other men; including her father, who had abandoned her. Although she was fully aware that she'd given Henry herpes and had mentally as well as physically abused *him*, she was consumed by her tendency to play the role of the victim. In her mind, it was she who had been wronged. Nevertheless her intense need to have a man in her life overrode her pride and rationality. However, despite her pleas Henry's mind was made up. He was bound and determined to get away from this psycho whore who he'd tried so desperately to save. So with her laying flat on her stomach with her hands wrapped around his legs, he dragged her all the way outside to his red Ford pickup truck. Dora's boys: Lane and Luke; who were out in the yard playing, watched their mother as she tried miserably to dissuade Henry from leaving. This was something that they were used to seeing because they were subjected to their mother's dysfunctional relationships frequently. Nevertheless they became consumed with fear and the anticipation of what was to come because when Dora didn't have a boyfriend, she did terrible things to them. And since Henry had been around, Dora didn't do the sadistic things that she did to them when it was just the three of them. Plus they genuinely liked Henry because he was nice to them, unlike all of Dora's other boyfriends.

When Henry finally reached the door of his truck it took every ounce of strength he had to pry Dora's hands off his leg. He had to almost choke her to the point of unconsciousness just to weaken her grip. When she finally had no choice but to loosen her hold on him he pushed her to the ground, slammed the door and squealed tires, leaving a trail of dust in the air.

Dora laid on the ground crying and screaming as she watched his truck disappear down the street. When his truck was finally out of her eyesight, she sat up, looked around and wiped her face. Suddenly her mood changed from despair to sheer calmness. As if in a trance, she got up like nothing had happened, smoothed out her bright red t-shirt and walked back towards the house. She peered over at the boys with an ominous stare and told them to go take baths. As they gathered their toys from off the ground, they subconsciously began to brace themselves because Dora's look foreshadowed what was yet to come.

Dora went into the house and picked up the phone. She dialed Henry's number and left several messages. The first set of messages was those by which she cried and pleaded for him to come back and forgive her. The next set was more vulgar with her calling him everything but the child of God. After she grew tired of calling Henry, she made a few other phone calls in hopes of reaching one of her old boyfriends. Once she was done making phone calls, she went into her room and pulled out a black lace negligee that Henry had given to her. As she put it on her pale white body, she laughed a wicked laugh to herself and thought, "Well Henry you bastard, if you don't want me, I know somebody who will."

She smeared on bright red lipstick, combed her thick dirty blonde hair and admired herself in the mirror. The rough skin and sunken eyes that had developed as a result of the way she'd lived her life didn't faze her because to her, she was the sexiest damn woman alive. She squirted on some of her favorite perfume and sashayed over to her bed where she laid down with her legs spread eagle style. She was ready to move on and let go of that good for nothing Henry. "Who the hell did he think he was anyway? He couldn't just leave her." She thought to herself as she began to fondle herself seductively. Just as she began to feel warm and moist in preparation of what was to come, she heard a faint knock on the door.

"I'm ready. Come on in." She replied. The door slowly opened and Dora's seven year old twin boys, Luke and Lane reluctantly walked into the room. They were both scantily clad in a pair of black boxer shorts that hung from their slightly malnourished bodies. Luke had curly blonde hair like his mother while Lane had a head full of dark brown curls that were assumed to be like that of his unknown father's. Both boys had inherited their mother's sky blue eyes and pale white skin tone.

"You boys come on in here and do what you know mama loves for you to do. Luke it's your turn to take the top and Lane, honey, you take real good care of mommy's bottom parts. Hurry up now and take your clothes off." She ordered in a comforting "motherly" voice as if she was coaching them to clean their rooms. They however, were desensitized to anything "motherly" that their mother said or did because Dora's "motherliness" was so inconsistent and unpredictable. They never knew if she would be hugging them or hurting. Nevertheless they followed her orders and began to slowly remove their boxer shorts. Although they were disgusted with whatever capacity a seven year old mind could be disgusted; their mother's frequent exploitation of their ability to refuse her treachery had taught them to become callous to her advances. They were now well aware that every time that their mother was in between men, they would have to pick up the slack. They had become men in ways that no seven year old boy should ever have to experience. Dora had taught them both how to please a woman in more ways than one. They knew how to, according to Dora, "dine on fine southern cuisine and suck on breasts like a new born baby." She had them switch roles on each "occasion" so that they both would be precise in relishing all areas of the female body.

"Luke, come here and kiss me baby." She said in an attempt to make her cigarette parched voice sound sexy. Luke who was the more rebellious twin walked up to her with the look of repugnance and hate on his face. In his head he saw himself biting down so hard onto Dora's nipple that it detached from her breast. Oblivious to his look, Dora moaned out, "Touch me and rub on my breasts just like I taught you to do."And he did as he was told but he wanted so badly to hurt his mother. He wanted to humiliate her but he restrained himself because he was fully aware of Dora's method of retaliation. Therefore, based on his better judgment he knew that he'd better submit to her demands or suffer the consequences. Lane; who was the timid twin, had already assumed his position and was doing everything within his little seven year old body to make Dora reach what she called, "her climax" so that she would leave them alone.

"Ohhhhh, Lane, lick faster and put more pressure on my clit like I taught you to. Ohhhh, yes, yes. You boys are sooooo good. You're getting ready to make mommy have an orgasm." Tears rolled down Lane's face as he caressed his mother and performed oral sex on her. Her putrid smell and sloppy juices penetrated his nose and sloshed all over his face. He felt the strong urge to vomit but knew that if he did she would burn him with cigarettes and pull off his toenails like she had the last time.

Monday Morning: Carolyn Black

I sat at my desk catching up on some paperwork, my cell phone rang. I answered it and it was Brad.

"Hello Brad. How's it going?" I replied while changing my voice from professional into my "I want your body" sex kitten tone.

"Carolyn, hey gorgeous, how are you today?"

"I'm fine Brad, just catching up on some paper work." I started to get excited because I knew Brad only called when there was some sort of extravagant event taking place that I knew I would be asked to accompany him on. I had been seeing Brad for about 8 months and he never ceased to amaze me.

"Well I was just calling to see if you would like to go with me to Colorado to do some skiing and enjoy the breath taking scenery. I'm going to be out there for about three days doing a little business but for you it will be all pleasure. So what do ya say?"

I didn't want to seem desperate so I played with him a little bit and made it seem as if I had other plans. Once I'd "checked my schedule" and made sure that it was clear I "gave in" knowing that I was going before he could even get the words out. He told me that he would have my plane ticket ready for me at the airport. And since I was off on Fridays I could fly to Colorado Friday morning and meet him at the hotel. As he was getting off the phone, I heard a female voice in the background that referred to him as "honey" and I assumed that it was his wife Angie. And by the way he coolly got off the phone with me; I knew my assumption was right. I laughed to myself and thought, "Humph, if she only knew".

That weekend, I went on the trip with Brad and had an awesome time. Of course I came home with lavish gifts and another unimaginable experience that I could add to my list. That is, my list of great places I'd been and extraordinary things I'd done courtesy of someone else's funding. Upon return on that Sunday evening, Dewayne called and wanted me to come spend time with him during the upcoming weekend at a hotel where the NC Association of Cardiologists was having a weeklong conference. I, of course accepted. I knew it was kind of trifling to be with a different man within less than a week span but I didn't care. There had been times when I was with a man on Monday and a different one on Wednesday. As long as I had time to soak in some vinegar and tighten my girl back up, I really didn't worry about it.

I worked the week out with no major problems or CPS reports and prepared myself to meet with Dewayne on Friday afternoon. I arrived at the lavish hotel that resembled a castle and went to get my room key. Dewayne was very smart and always made sure to get two rooms, one of which he paid cash for. When I got to my room, there was a box lying on the bed with a beautiful navy blue teddy inside it. I was a little disappointed until he knocked on the door and came in holding another box. This one was much smaller so I automatically knew that it had to be jewelry. He handed it to me and inside was a necklace with a single diamond and a pair of one karat diamond earrings. I hugged him and told him how much I appreciated the gifts. He smiled and asked me to have a seat. I enjoyed spending time with Dewayne because we talked like too old friends and politicked about this and that. Dewayne was just that kind of guy. He was old school and treated me like a lady. He never wanted to come in and immediately start having sex. He was nice and always wanted to talk. I guess that's what he was missing with his wife. Plus it didn't hurt that he was very nice looking with chocolate brown skin, coal black eyes and curly black hair. He stood about five foot nine, 190 lbs and looked every bit of forty years old although he was fifty.

After we talked, he ordered room service, we ate and then I took a shower. I put on the lingerie he'd bought for me and sashayed out to model for him. Of course he was very impressed with my voluptuous but tight physique. He touched and teased me before we eventually made love and fell asleep. The remainder of the weekend I was alone with the exception of our "night caps." Dewayne was very cautious and did not want to risk being seen with me. But he definitely spared no expense because I got the full spa treatment and ate whatever I wanted at the full service restaurant inside the hotel. Yes I was alone for the majority of the day but it didn't bother me because I was being well compensated.

On Sunday as I was going to get breakfast prior to checking out, I walked into the restaurant and noticed Dewayne sitting at a table with a woman. She was very regal and exuded an air of arrogance. She had her dark brown hair pulled into a tight chignon at the nape of her neck. She wore a cream blouse with black slacks and pearl earrings. She had beautiful caramel brown skin and thick black eyebrows. She appeared to be very petite with small beady black eyes. I assumed that she was a colleague of Dewayne's until I saw the look on his face when he noticed me walking in. I briefly stopped in my tracks but quickly regained my composure. At that point I knew it was his wife and therefore got my food to go.
As I was waiting on my food, I began to feel a little devilish. I'd noticed that there was a table with a young and very hot doctor sitting there who had been checking me out since I came in. In a fit of retaliation, I began flirting with him with my eyes. He eventually asked me to join him and I obliged. I had no intentions of having my breakfast with him but I did want to see how Dewayne would

react. I knew I was dead wrong because I knew the rules of the game but a pang of animosity overrode our covenant. I laughed and giggled with the young doctor but I watched as Dewayne squirmed out of the corner of my eye. I could tell that he was very uncomfortable; not with me and his wife being in the same room, but more so with my interaction with the young doctor. The more he squirmed the more I enjoyed myself. "How dare he disrupt me from enjoying my breakfast and treat me like a low class prostitute." I thought to myself. I knew that I was in fact his mistress but deep down inside I was jealous and a little taken aback that I had to remain hidden all weekend. At least with Brad he did take me out in public. No I didn't want Dewayne on a relationship level, I just felt like I was entitled to more than being secluded in a hotel room.

When my food arrived, I made sure to visibly get the young doctor's number and then sashayed back to my room. I knew that I looked stunning in my canary yellow halter dress that hugged my curves. I wore my hair curly and wild and sported a new glow courtesy of the spa treatment that I'd received. As I walked to the elevator, I knew that Dewayne would be beyond pissed but I really didn't give a damn. I also knew that Dewayne had been more than generous to me but I didn't give a damn about that either. I thought to myself, "No man, and I repeat, no man will ever downgrade Carolyn Black to a second class mistress. I am `the other woman,' no more, but definitely no less."

When I got to work on Monday morning after my rendezvous' with Brad and Dewayne, Valerie laughed at me because she knew how adventurous my past few days had been. I always let her know when and where I was going so somebody would know where I was just in case something happened. She called me into her office and shut the door. She asked for all the details which I sparingly gave to her because I didn't want her to know too much. Val at times attempted to live vicariously through me and my wild life because her life was so ordinary. But she didn't know that I would have traded all the crap I was doing for a normal, happy life in a minute. I showed her the diamond earrings that

Dewayne had given me and she oooooed and awwwwed in envy. We laughed and giggled but deep down inside I felt no happiness or joy, I simply felt gratification.

Thursday morning: Lane and Luke

Lane sat in class with his mouth burning and a cold sore the size of a dime on his lip. His mother had been applying ointment to it, but it just wouldn't go away. The teacher sent him to the school nurse who took one look at the cold sore on his lip and the ones inside of his mouth and knew that something wasn't quite right. The nurse called Lane's mother and recommended that Lane go to the hospital immediately to get checked out. Dora reluctantly picked Lane and his brother up from school and took Lane to the doctor. On the way there she warned him that if he said anything about their "secret games" then all of his toenails would be removed one by one. However, when the doctor examined Lane and found that Lane had Herpes around his mouth, it didn't take long for the doctor to automatically recognize that when a seven year old had herpes around and inside his mouth, something terrible was going on. Therefore the doctor immediately called Fosterberg County Department of Social Services.

Carolyn Black

"Hi mom, how's it going?" I asked as I initiated my daily conversation with my mother. I had just arrived at work and was settling in at my desk.

"Hi baby, I'm doing good trying to get your father out the door. You know how he is." She replied. I, knowing mother, knew that she was shaking her head or rolling eyes with a gentle smile on her face at the mention of my father.

"Well make sure you give him some kisses for me."

"You know I will. Are you coming over for your sister Sylvia's birthday cookout?" She asked, knowing that I loathed attending anything whereby my sisters would be present.

"Do I have a choice?" I mumbled, knowing that I didn't. If I didn't go, they would talk crap about me because I wasn't there and if I did go then they would chastise me for the way I was dressed or how I had my hair or just because they were two wicked heifers that thrived off making my life miserable.

"Carolyn, I don't know why you and your sisters don't get along. You all are family and y'all should be good to each other." Not wanting to be a snitch and run to "my mommy" about what was really going on with the way *they* treated me, I held it in and just agreed with her.

As we were talking, I got a call from the intake worker about a report that had been made from the hospital. I gladly accepted the interruption and told my mom that I would call her back. I got the demographic information and due to the referral coming from the hospital, I immediately dropped what I was doing and headed straight there.

As soon as I arrived at Fosterberg Medical Center, I prepared myself for what I might be walking into. I showed my badge to the lady at the front desk and got directions to where I was supposed to go. I met with a doctor who handed me a written report and began to brief me. But before he could really discuss what was going on, he got a page and had to leave. As he walked out the door, he told me where I could find the child and his mother and promised to rejoin me as soon as he could.

I flipped the chart open and started skimming through the report. When I saw that it was about a seven year old child that had herpes around his mouth, my first thought was, "What the hell?" "A seven year old with herpes around his mouth? Shoot poor baby probably used the wrong person's toothbrush or something. Mother probably parties too much and has a bunch of people in and out of her house and the child has come into contact with somebody or something used by the wrong person. Yes! This is going to be easy. In and out." I summarized to myself, thinking about the big stack of paperwork I had lying on my desk. I closed the folder and headed to where the mother was sitting in the waiting room nearby. When I walked in I saw a pale, scantily clad, skeleton of a woman sitting in a chair with her legs crossed shaking them nervously. She wore thickly caked, green eye shadow and hot pink lipstick. She had beautiful sky blue eyes and thick dirty blonde hair. She probably had been a very pretty woman at one time in her life but now she looked as if a combination of moonshine and hard knocks had taken their toll on her. Sitting beside her was a cute little boy who had curly blonde hair and eyes just as breathtaking as his mothers.

"Dora, Dora Brown?" I asked politely as I held my hand out to shake hers.

"Um, yes I'm Dora Brown. How can I help you?"She replied warmly with a deep scratchy voice, as she accepted my hand.

"My name is Carolyn Black and I'm with the Fosterberg County Department of Social Services. " Her face immediately turned pale white. And her hand, which was weakly gripping mine, began to sweat. I quickly let go of her hand because the thought of another person's sweat on me; besides that of a man, was disgusting. I knew she was probably nervous and confused as were all parents who were approached by someone stating, "Hi, I'm from the Department of Social Services." I turned my attention to the little boy who was looking right at me.

"Is this your son as well?" I asked.

"Yes he is." Dora replied.

"Hello, young man. My name is Carolyn. How are you?" I asked, opting to put my hands on my knees and squat down to his eye level instead of shaking his hand.

"Fine." He replied, in a calm and reserved manner, never taking his eyes off me. Our eyes locked and being that his were so blue and clear, his gaze entrapped me for a second.

"And what is your name?"

"Luke." He replied, still looking directly at me.

"And how old are you Luke?"

"Seven." He answered boldly.

"Well, it's nice to meet you Luke." I replied.

"Wow that was weird." I thought to myself as I stood up and turned around; only to meet Dora's now icy blue eyes, glaring at me. "Damnit! What the hell."I thought to myself, almost jumping out of my skin because I wasn't prepared for *those* eyes and *that* look. But I quickly regained my composure. And noticing the change in her countenance, I recognized that she was upset. So I motioned for her to walk with me across the room so that we could have some privacy.

I asked, "Ms. Brown, are you ok?"

"Uh, yes, I'm fine but why has Social Services been called here?" She asked leaning against the wall as her short red sundress drooped off her bony shoulders.

"Well, I got a report from the hospital stating that your son, Lane Brown, has Herpes I and II in and around his mouth. It's just hospital policy for them to call us."

"Do you have any idea how your son got Herpes around his mouth?" I asked.

"Now why would you think that I know something about it?" Dora asked, becoming unnecessarily defensive. In my effort to try and stay professional, I took a deep breath. I was used to dealing with parents who displayed a variety of different emotions so I decided to change my approach.

"Ma'am, your son has Herpes around his mouth and it's not just fever blisters. I have to do my job and find out what happened. There is no need for you to get upset; I just need your help."

She crossed her arms and squinted her icy blue eyes. "Like I said, how would I know? They play outside all the time, they run around all the time; they're in and out of stuff all the time. I'm not around them every single fucking minute. He could've got it from anywhere." She snapped.

I was bewildered by this woman's sudden change in mood and level of defensiveness. Not to mention her disregard for the real reason I was here and that being her son. Her son, who at seven had a STD that he would have for the rest of his life. I saw no tears; I saw no compassion, only anger. I wasn't here to take her children away. I was here to find out whose toothbrush the kid may have used, take a few pictures and head back to the office and finish my work. In fact, she probably was the culprit and didn't want to admit it. It was probably *her* toothbrush that her son had used.

Making one more attempt to reach her on her level, I asked, "Ms. Brown is there anyone residing in your home or who has been to your home that may have Herpes?"

"How the hell should I know? I don't go around administering STD tests. You ask too many damn questions lady. Now can I take my kids home?"

"No ma'am you can't. Not until I do my job."

I knew I wasn't going to get anywhere with her because she was too defensive. So I decided to go and talk to her son.

"I'll be back after I talk to Lane." I said. Giving me the evil eye, she reluctantly walked over and sat down beside her other son. I made a mental note to have her tested for STD's just to be on the safe side.

"How long are you gonna be in there?" She asked as I was turning to walk away.

"Hopefully not long. " I replied. I walked down the hall and found the hospital room where her other son, Lane was sitting on the hospital bed; waiting. He was so cute that I just wanted to squeeze his cheeks. He resembled his brother a lot because he had those same beautiful blue eyes. However, he had big locks of curly brown hair and he was a lot smaller in frame than his brother. He also was more sheepish and anxious than his brother. He made as little eye contact as possible and kept his head down.

"Hi Lane, my name is Carolyn Black. I am a Social Worker and I came to talk to you about why you're in the hospital." I said extending my hand only because I knew I had to make him feel a little more comfortable. He gave me his hand but continued looking down. "Wow, they are like day and night." I thought to myself, referring to Luke and Lane.

"Lane it's ok, this will be over quicker than you know it." As he looked up at me to get reassurance that things were really going to be ok, I got a chance to look into *his* beautiful blue eyes, which were full of sadness and fear. "Wow." I thought to myself. "Three sets of the same blue eyes, all telling a different story but with a common theme: fear and distrust.

"How old are you Lane?" I asked.

"Seven." He whispered. "Twins? Wow. They are so incredibly different." I thought to myself.

"Have you ever been in the hospital before?"

"No." He responded, still looking down.

"Well, I want to talk to you for a little bit about what's going on with your mouth. Did the doctor tell you what was wrong?"

"No." He replied softly.

"Well, the doctor said that you have Herpes in and around your mouth and its very unusual for a seven year old to have this form of Herpes around the mouth because that's a very grown up disease." He didn't respond but he began squirming around and tugging at his shirt. I could tangibly see the anxiety that he was feeling, which alarmed me. I just didn't understand why he was so afraid but I chalked it up to him being nervous about being in the hospital talking to a bunch of strangers.

"Lane, you don't have to be afraid ok. This is a very simple procedure that will not take that long. Now once we find out a few more things you will be able to go home with your family. Now I'm going to have to ask you to open your mouth real wide so I can take pictures." He did as he was told but with reluctance. After I took pictures of his mouth, I pushed the buzzer and asked the nurse to come in with me so we could continue discussing the report since the doctor had not yet returned. As the nurse was walking in, I heard his mother in the hallway ranting and raving.

"What the hell is going on in there with my son? I'm coming in there. You ain't gonna be in there with my son without me." The poor nurse was trying her best to calm Dora down and discuss the process that had to be conducted in these types of situations. But I, on the other hand, had had enough of that woman and the *Carolyn Black* in me began to take over my professionalism. So I walked past the nurse and got straight in Dora's face and said, "Ms. Brown, let me tell you something, if you don't sit down and close your mouth I will call the police on you and have you arrested. So I suggest you calm down and let us do our job. Everything we're doing is routine. We are not going to endanger your child and if you haven't done anything wrong then you don't have anything to worry about, ok?"

And when she looked in my face and saw that I was serious she sat down and didn't say another word.

"Don't let this pretty white woman face fool you." I thought to myself.

I walked back into the room with Lane and picked up the folder so that I could thoroughly review the report. As I read into more detail, I noted that the teacher had voiced several concerns regarding the boys' behavior, tiredness, poor academic performance and refusal to play with any of the other children. The teacher had also mentioned other things that she was concerned about; however, it was the last sentence that made me sigh. The words, "suspected abuse but I have no proof" let me know that the pile of paperwork on my desk would probably be sitting there for the rest of the day. I turned to look at Lane, who was still looking down, fidgeting with his shirt. I gave him a good look over to see if I noticed anything that raised a red flag. He seemed to be ok but I did notice that his socks were disgustingly dirty and I could not stand to see a child in dirty clothes, shoes or anything else.

"Trifling, heifer." I thought to myself, referring to Dora. I turned to the nurse and asked her if she could bring some hospital socks in for Lane to wear until he got home. When the nurse returned, I handed the socks to Lane and told him to put them on. He froze and fixated his stare on the socks.

"Lane, honey I need you to put those socks on please. The ones you have on are very dirty and can cause you to have a fungus." I said, not understanding his reaction. "This family is crazy." I thought to myself.

Lane didn't move, with the exception of his shaky hands. Then I noticed sweat running down his face. "What the hell?" I thought to myself. I walked over and sat down on the bed beside him. I reached out to put my hand on his back, but his body jerked forward before I could barely make contact with him.

"Lane honey, what's wrong?"

"I can't take off my socks; I can't take off my socks." He said, beginning to tremble.

"Why baby? Why can't you take off your socks?" I asked gently.

"I can't, I can't." He said, becoming hysterical. The nurse and I both tried to comfort him but based on his reaction, I knew I was going to have to take his socks off for him. I knew he was hiding something and I had no choice to find out what it was.

I saw a box of gloves sitting on the counter and went to retrieve a pair. I walked back over to Lane, squatted down and proceeded to take off his socks.

"No, no, no!" He said; squirming around, beginning to get hysterical. Knowing that I only had a small amount of time before he really flipped out, I jerked the socks off and threw them on the floor. When I looked down at his feet, I realized why he was so upset. Out of 10 toes, only four of them had toenails still attached. There were no scratches or cuts or remaining pieces to the toe nails that had been pulled off which led me to believe that someone had taken something and simply pulled them off. The nurse and I looked at each other in dismay. Lane, who was now full blown hysterical, cried uncontrollably.

"She's gonna kill me, she's gonna kill me, she's gonna kill me." He began reciting in the midst of hyperventilating.

"Lane baby, no one is going to kill you. Who did this to you? What happened?"

As if in a trance, he continued to repeat the words, "she's gonna kill me, she's gonna kill me." The nurse sat down beside Lane and began trying to comfort him. I, on the other hand, took a deep breath because in my heart I feared that the "she" that Lane was referring to was his mother. At that point I *knew* that I wasn't leaving anytime soon because I was now going to have to conduct a full blown investigation. I was actually glad that I had made Lane take his socks off because if I hadn't, then I would have let him go home with his mother or to whomever this, "she" was. I took another deep sigh because I had to think and figure out how to proceed. I knew that if Lane was being abused, Luke was probably being abused as well so I knew I had to get Luke in the room so that I could examine him as well. The problem was Dora and keeping her from acting a fool in the hospital. Thinking quickly, I concocted a plan. I went out and told Dora that Lane wanted his brother Luke to come in with him so that he would be more comfortable. Technically I wasn't telling a lie because I did feel that Lane would calm down some with his brother in the room.

Dora, who was becoming more agitated, objected until I gave her "the look." She mouthed off at me and made idle threats but she reluctantly allowed him to go. When Luke and I returned to the room, I had Luke to sit in the reclining chair while I went and gently sat down on the bed beside Lane. I knew that the remaining part of my investigation was going to be difficult but I was glad that the two of them could lean on each other.

I started the investigation by taking pictures of Lane's toes. Once again I asked him what had happened to his toes and who this mysterious "she" was and once again he refused to answer. But Luke, who was more verbal and fearless, answered for him. "Dora did it. She makes us do stuff to her. She calls them our secret games." The color slowly drained from Lane's small face as Luke described the things Dora made them do to her and how she would react if they refused. Apparently, Lane had refused; therefore resulting in him loosing toenails. I was sickened. In all my years of being a CPS worker, I had never heard such a horrifying story.

"What kind of mother turned her own son's into her personal sex slaves?" I was so furious that I wanted to go out into the waiting room and beat the shit out of her but I maintained my composure for the boys. As I was jotting down notes, preparing to continue the investigation, the doctor walked in. I pulled him to the side and talked with him about what Luke had just told me. And he; just as I and the nurse, was disgusted and in disbelief that a mother could do such heinous things.

After filling the doctor in, I took what seemed to be my hundredth deep breath and proceeded with the investigation.

"Lane, I'm sorry to have to do this but I need you to take your shirt off because I have to check over the rest of your body for marks, bruises or anything else. I promise I won't hurt you and I will try to make this go as quickly as possible." I said as soothingly as I could. But as I walked towards him, he scurried to the head of the bed and balled up into a fetal position.

"No! I don't want to. Please don't make me, please don't make me." He said fearfully, beginning to tremble again. I wanted to pick him up and wrap him in my arms but my self imposed boundaries: no touching the children intimately, no getting attached to the children and remain poise at all times, stopped me. Nevertheless on the inside my heart was breaking. It was obvious that the child was petrified.

"Lane, I'm sorry. I really hate that I have to do this but there is no other way." At that point he began sobbing and shaking uncontrollably. And nothing that I could do or say would calm him down. But his brother Luke got up, walked over to Lane, took his hand and said, "It's going to be alright, I'm here."He then jumped up on the bed and put his arms around his fragile brother. He laid Lane's head onto his small chest and began rocking him. I just stood there watching, mesmerized; unable to speak. The way Luke comforted his brother with such ease and effortlessness made me think that this was routine for him; for the both of them.

Leaving them in the nurse's care, I stepped into the bathroom to call my supervisor, Valerie. I told her everything I knew and informed her that those boys could not return home with their mother. She agreed and told me that she would call a team decision making meeting (TDM) to discuss having them placed in a temporary foster home until we could get them into a more permanent placement.

After talking with Valerie, I contacted the police department and relayed the information to them. I told them to come quickly because I knew that the longer we kept the boys in the room, there was a great chance that Dora was going to become hostile and turn the hospital out. I personally didn't even want to look at her so I didn't go tell her that I knew what was going on. Plus there was nothing left to say anyway so I figured that I would let the police deal with her. When the police arrived, I assume that her guilt got the best of her because she immediately became irate without even knowing why they were there. They weren't going to arrest her until I gave them a full report, nevertheless she kept yelling, "you ain't gonna take my kids! Bring my boys out here to me now!" She became so loud and out of control that she was eventually escorted outside of the hospital thus giving me the opportunity to continue my investigation without her presence. Once they knew that she was gone they both seemed to be relieved and let all the things they'd held trapped up in their little minds, flow like a river. I assured them that they were safe and no one else could harm them. They eventually loosened up and both let me take pictures of their bodies. When the nurse, the doctor and I saw the cigarette burns on their backs and bottoms as well as the little toes that were missing toenails, we all exchanged looks of shock. Once my shock wore off, I became enraged. I wanted to take Dora out into a field, tie her up, pull off *her* toenails, burn her body all over with cigarettes and then beat her to a bloody pulp.

After thoroughly examining them and taking their statements, I took the report to the remaining police officer who was standing out in the hallway. After viewing the pictures that I'd taken, he immediately went and arrested Dora and charged her with felony child abuse. The doctor wanted to keep both boys at the hospital so that he could do a thorough medical exam so I returned to the office; promising to pick them up once he was done.

The team and I all got together for the TDM meeting and made arrangements to have the boys placed in a temporary foster home. I also made a referral for extensive outpatient therapy services because I knew that with all those boys had been through, they were definitely going to need it. Once I got the all clear from the doctor, I picked them up and transported them to the temporary placement I'd set up for them.

Once I'd gotten the boys placed safely in one of our licensed foster homes, I took a final sigh and thought about how much wine and weed I was going to need in order to settle my nerves. I figured that I needed a big tall glass of wine and about three blunts.

But luckily for me as I was walking to my car, something better came along; a big tall glass of Demarcus.

"What's up?" Came his deep sexy voice through the phone. I automatically started smiling like I was in high school. I knew I was blushing and my body melted all over.

"Hey Demarcus. How are you?"

"Fine baby. You still off on Friday's?" He asked.

"Yep, you know it." I replied.

"Well I been missing you and *she* in jail for thirty days on some of her regular bullshit. My son's grandmother has got him this weekend so I was hoping that I could come see you." In my mind I laughed at how he always referred to his wife as "she," never stating her name. I on the other hand like to refer to her as "the hood rat."

"Oh my gosh Demarcus, you are sooo just what the doctor ordered." I replied, grinning even wider.

"Why wus going on babe? You having a bad day at work?"

"You just wouldn't believe it if I told you boo." I answered shaking my head.

"Well how soon will you be home?" He asked.

"I'm on my way now."

"Well I will stop and get us some wine and some take out and I will be over there in about an hour. Then you can tell me all about it. I have to tell you about this dumb ass bitch too but that can wait until later. I'll see you in a little bit."

"Ok baby. See ya in a little bit." I replied as I hung up. I got in my car and headed home. I was overwhelmed by what I had just experienced with those little boys. I shook my head because regardless of how long I had been on this job, the things that people did to children never ceased to amaze me. I had been getting better at not taking my job home with me but sometimes, in certain situations I couldn't help but cry. On this particular occasion, had it not been for that sexy voice soothing my angst I would have definitely taken it home with me tonight. But I knew that I was in for a treat by spending time with Demarcus Not just because of the anticipated juicy hot sex, but stress relief and great conversation as well. That is what made me hate Demarcus and love him so much at the same time. I knew that I could dump my whole day of trash on him and he would take it, bag it up and throw it away for me. I knew that we would eat; smoke weed and talk into the wee hours of the night. The sex would simply be the icing on the cake. But just like the other men in my boudoir, he was married and I knew that he would only be mine for a short time. The difference was that he was really the only one that I had genuine emotions for and he was the only one of my men who actually knew where I lived.

It had been a long time since I had seen him and I was ecstatic because he was all mine for the weekend. He arrived with wine, Italian food and a fat sack of weed; all of which he knew were my favorites. He greeted me with a hug and let me release all my sorrows from the events that had occurred earlier that day. Of course I, being professional, didn't release any identifying information about the boys but the things I could talk about rolled off my tongue relentlessly. He rubbed my feet as I talked, shook his head and listened to what those poor boys had had to endure at the hands of their mother. And then, he ran me a hot bath, bathed me and made love to me all night long. The next morning, I laid there looking at him as he slept. I wanted him to belong to me so badly but I knew that he would never be mine. As tears began to well up in my eyes, I rolled over so I wouldn't have to look at him. But as soon as he felt me roll over, he grabbed me and wrapped his arms around me. Although it felt so good being in his arms, I didn't want to lose control of my emotions and tease myself with false hope. I couldn't handle knowing that I was only experiencing momentary intimacy so I rebelliously broke out of his embrace and climbed on top of him. I began kissing him and licking his chest. I bit his nipples and made my way down to his manhood. He was the only man who got "special attention" from me and it was a rare delicacy even for him. But my mind was cloudy and I needed a quick distraction. So I closed my eyes and sucked as I detached myself from the perilous intimacy that he'd attempted to bestow upon me. I became lost in thought and reflected back over the charade that characterized Demarcus and I's relationship.

I never got tired of Demarcus' sex because it was so damn good but sometimes when we got together we didn't even have sex because we were too busy laughing and talking. And when we did have sex, he never just got up and left after making love to me. We always basked in the afterglow and held each other while we talked. He was always interested in the things that were going on in my life as was I about the things going on in his. These things were confusing for me and threatened to relinquish the limited control that I attempted to grasp each time I was in his presence. I knew that he would never split up his family; nevertheless I kept going back to our fantasy world hence reigniting the ring of fire that threatened to melt the self imposed ice block I held around my heart. Sometimes I imagined that Demarcus and I shared the same feelings because of the way he looked at me. I often wished that he and I had committed to each other a long time ago before he had gotten involved with the Hood Rat. My relationship with Demarcus was symbolic of an ominous calamity. It was an ongoing battle whereby the contenders were my desire and intense hope versus my dignity and stalwart opposition of love; with the latter being compromised and at risk of defeat because of the stronghold Demarcus held over me.

"Ohhhh myyyy God, Carolyn, you about to make me cum!" Demarcus screamed out, distracting me from my thoughts; catapulting me back into the present. Nevertheless his cry for mercy didn't stop me. It only made me more relentless within my internal battle to make him succumb to my power, and I didn't care that it would only be a temporary victory. I sucked harder, took him in deeper and moaned loudly as if I were a porn star. No longer able to withstand the carnal punishment that I'd bestowed upon him, he vehemently grabbed two handfuls of my hair and came hard in my mouth. When he was done, I gave him a malicious but naughty girl look and swallowed his babies without taking my eyes off him. I then got up without saying a word and sashayed to the bathroom to brush my teeth. "Yeah." I thought to myself. "And the win goes to...me; Carolyn Black."

After I finished brushing my teeth, I came back into the

bedroom to find Demarcus lying on the bed trying to catch his breath. I laughed to myself again at the victory I'd just won and laid down on the bed beside him. I made a conscious effort not to touch him because I knew that if I did then my past efforts would be in vain.

"Damn Carolyn. Shit. What got into you?"

"What are you talking about?" I asked innocently.

"You know exactly what I'm talking about Superhead." He replied. I laughed, despite myself and rolled over without responding. He then got up and went to the bathroom where I heard him relieving himself. When he returned, I was still lying on my side, naked from our rendezvous'. He crept up on me as if I was a gazelle and he was a tiger, going in for the prey. He jerked me by my legs to the bottom of the bed and forcefully spread them open. Caught off guard I tried to retreat back to the top of the bed thus igniting a battle of cat and mouse; controller versus controlee.

"Did you think it was just going to go down like that Carolyn Black? Open up them thick white legs and let me play with what's inside em." He said as he interlocked his strong dark arms around my legs; creating the look of an ice cream swirl.

I continued fighting, squirming and resisting advances; all in vain because my legs were locked in his arms. And before I knew it he was savoring my Juicy and I was melting on his face. Just as I was about to scream out in ecstasy, he stopped abruptly and rammed his manhood inside me; sending me into a catastrophic ambivalence. I didn't want to cum and allow him to win but my body was riveting in orgasmic seizures that were so strong that I could no longer withhold the inevitable. I came hard. The orgasm was so intense that I dug my claws into his back and screamed to the top of my lungs. He, being just as competitive as I, was also relentless and kept pounding me until he reached his climax. After the war was over, he and I both lay on the bed breathless, huffing and puffing as if we'd just run a marathon. Neither of us spoke for what seemed like an eternity.

Breaking the silence, he said, "Damn, I think we need to smoke a blunt after that." Unable to hold sustain my "I am woman, hear me roar" stance any longer, I burst out laughing. He always knew how to make me laugh in an uncomfortable situation.

"Well there's still a half of one in the ash tray, go ahead and spark it up." I replied in between giggles as my guard slowly began to descend.

"Cool," He said as he went to retrieve our much anticipated third party.

"Here, I think you most definitely won the right to take the first pull." He said with a sheepish smile as he handed me my home girl, Mary Jane. I lit her up and took a long, slow pull. The smoke filled my lungs and my mind with clouds. I savored the feeling, not wanting to release the smoke back into the air. But I had to relinquish because I started coughing profusely and couldn't stop. Knowing the, "puff, puff, pass rule", I handed the blunt to Demarcus, who was delighted by my compromised "advanced smoker skills."

"Now I'ma show you how to smoke, baby lungs." He said, playfully snatching the blunt out of my hand. In an attempt to challenge me, he took an over exaggeratedly long, drawn out pull and held his breath. With cockiness in his eyes, he tried to endure the thick smoke that antagonized his lungs. Failing miserably; not only did he let the smoke out, he started hacking so hard that tears were rolling down his face. Tears also rolled down *my face* as I *rolled* around on the bed laughing at him. I laughed so hard that my ribs ached. He fell back on the bed and joined me in laughing.

Finishing up the blunt, he asked, "Whatchu got to eat in there?"

"There's a lot of stuff in there. You know I keep my refrigerator stocked at all times. Why? What you got a taste for?" He looked at me with a mischievous look and replied, "Besides you, I would love to cook you a Demarcus style breakfast with bacon, eggs and homemade waffles."

"Ok." I laughed as I moved to get out of bed to show him around the kitchen. But before my feet could hit the floor, he stopped me and said, "No. You always cook for me. I want to cook for you. So you lay back and chill and let me make you breakfast in bed." Thrilled and unable to hide the largely growing smile on my face, I giggled and replied, "Ok."

As he navigated his way around the kitchen, I went to take a shower. Feeling clean and refreshed, I returned to my bedroom to find a naked Demarcus lying on the bed in between two trays of food. The room was delightfully scented with the aroma of syrup, waffles, bacon and the residue of sex. We ate, talked, smoked weed and watched movies. We didn't leave the bedroom any that day or the next with the exception of tending to our basic needs. As we were lying in bed early Sunday morning, he announced that he would have to leave soon because he had to go and pick up his son. I got quiet because I didn't want him to go. This was the longest amount of time that we had spent together in a long time and it felt so sweet and genuine. For once the emptiness that I always carried with me had temporarily disappeared.

He asked me why I had gotten quiet and I tried really hard to come up with an excuse that would not reveal my true feelings. But as if our thoughts were in conjunction with each other, he nodded at me without me having to say a word; signaling that he felt the same way. We both knew that our "vacation from reality" was over and we both would have to return to our normal lives. He kissed the brim of my nose and said, "Cee, I really need to tell you something. This has been messing with my head for a minute and I have got to get this off my chest."

My heart began to pound as he looked me in my eyes and said, "Cee, I love you and I've loved you since the first day we met. I ain't never been with a woman who makes me feel the way that you do. You are the most gangsta' ass chick that I know. You're smart, you're beautiful, you're sexy as hell, you hold it down and your ass can cook. Damn, man I..."He stopped midsentence and shook his head. My heart started pounding even harder when he reached over and grabbed my hand. I began salivating in anticipation. Was he getting ready to ask me to be his girl? Was he going to say that he wanted it to be just me and him?

He leaned in and gave me one of the most intense kisses I'd ever gotten in my life. "Oh my God, this is it." I squealed to myself like a teenage girl. "He's really getting ready to be my boyfriend." When the kiss was over, he leaned back and began to stroke my hair; never taking his eyes off mine.

"Damn Cee. I really want to be with you. I know we would make each other happy."My heart went into overdrive. "Yes! Hell Yea!" I thought to myself as I tried to conceal the overly excited expression threatening to spread across my face.

He took my hand, kissed it gently and locked his fingers into mine, never moving his eyes away from mine. With his other hand he started rubbing my face and then continued.

"But I can't leave my son and if I divorced *her* there's no way I would give her custody and I can't afford to take care of him by myself." The air began to slowly deflate out of my chest and the heart that was previously threatening to pound a hole through my chest now felt like it would simultaneously combust.

"High kill." I thought to myself trying to fight off my tears and mask my disappointment. I didn't know why I'd even wasted my time...or my heartbeat because I already knew he wasn't going to leave the hood rat because of his son. I knew I was setting myself up by allowing myself to even have an inkling of hope. Nevertheless, I wanted to fight for our love and declare that I would help take care of his son. But I knew I wasn't ready for kids and I also knew that no matter what we tried to do to make things work; they just weren't going to work.

I wrapped a sheet around myself, got up and walked into my sunroom. Of course he followed but I told him that he needed to get his things and leave. In my heart I really believed that he loved me but it hurt so bad because I knew that there was nothing that we could do about it. My love for him was destined to remain stagnant in my heart without the chance to grow and flourish. Although I had other lovers I would gladly leave all of them alone for him because he was the one person that truly understood me. That's why I tried to stay far away from him because he was like a drug. While I was on him, I was high in the sky but when I didn't have him, I crashed and burned. And constantly searched and yearned for that high to return to me in the same capacity.

As I watched him walk out the door, I ferociously fought back the tears that threatened to stream down my face. I wasn't going to let myself feel pain so I picked up the phone and called Jermaine. I told him to meet me in Boone NC in two hours. I showered, shed Demarcus off my body and headed to Boone to renew myself. As I drove I swore that I would never let him come near me again.

Case #32482: The Greatest Love

Tia Barksdale awoke from her three day crack binge to what she thought was the sound of a baby screaming at the top of its lungs. She sat straight up in the bed and scanned the room because, at that point, she had no recollection of who she was with or where she was. This was not an unfamiliar situation for Tia because on more than one occasion during similar crack binges, she had awakened in some very peculiar places totally oblivious to how she had gotten there or how long she'd been there. Luckily; this time, as she looked around she found that she was in her own small apartment in her own room. She continued scanning the room to see if anything was out of place or if there were any strange people scattered about because that was also something that was not out of the ordinary for her. Things were still hazy and her head pounded. The sound of the crying baby didn't help. Once she regained full consciousness she began to recognize the familiarity of the baby's cries. They were the cries of her one year old son Rob Jr.

"What is he doing here?" She thought to herself as she jumped up to go and see what was wrong with her baby. She was usually very careful not to have her son when she knew that she was going to be using. She usually only got high when he was with his father, Rob Sr. or the baby sitter. Lately she'd been more careless because her new boyfriend, Joey, was a drug dealer and he readily had crack for her on a daily basis. He regularly kept her doped up, which was not a problem for her because when she wasn't high she was itching to get high. The only problem was her son who she loved dearly and vowed to protect regardless of her craving to get high.

As she followed the cries which seemed to be coming from

the living room, she mentally kicked herself because she didn't know how long she'd been out of it and what kind of condition she would find her son in as a result of her negligence. When she got into the living room which she kept spotless clean, there was her boyfriend Joey standing over Rob Jr. with a wicked look on his face.

"Shut up, you little bastard before I really give you something to cry about." He hissed. Bewildered by Joey's harsh tone with the baby, Tia was halted in her tracks. She couldn't believe that this was the same man who acted as if he adored Rob Jr. when they were all together. She pinched herself because she thought that maybe she was dreaming or still high. But when she saw Joey smack Rob Jr. across the face because he wouldn't stop crying she knew that she wasn't dreaming. The mother bear in her came out and before she knew it, she grabbed a lamp and hit Joey across the back of the head with it.

She had been abused herself as a child and she'd be damned if she let that happen to her son. Although she knew she was a crack addict, she always did her best to make sure that her baby was safe and taken care of. But since Joey sold crack and always had it at his disposal it was harder for her to resist. Plus she really liked Joey because he had money and was very nice looking. He paid what little bills she had, bought her and Rob Jr. designer clothes and as mentioned, he kept her habit supplied. She knew that Joey had a temper but she never dreamed that he would take it out on a helpless baby. Yes she'd witnessed him getting angry at Rob Jr. for small things like making a mess or spilling things but never to this extremity. Or maybe because he constantly fed her with drugs she just hadn't noticed.

She picked the baby up and began to soothe him. Once he realized that he was in his mother's loving and safe arms, he began to calm down. Looking at her son in a more sober state of mind, she began to think and process things. She realized that Joey had been a little rougher with Rob Jr. then he should have been. In fact she remembered a time when he'd attempted to spank Rob Jr. but she'd stopped him. And the more and more she thought about it, she realized that she'd been allowing him to get away with doing things to Rob Jr. that she shouldn't have been. Angry and bound to make Joey pay, she started walking towards the phone so she could call the police but the thought of Joey going to jail and the probability of her having to start tricking again to feed her habit stopped her.

"I'll just keep a closer watch on him." She thought to herself as she hung up the phone. She looked down at Joey who was knocked out cold on the floor and then back at her precious baby. She let out a loud sob because she hated herself and Joey. She hated herself for being an addict and she hated Joey for what he was doing to her and her son. She knew that she would never be able to leave Joey as long as she was on crack because her crack addiction would overrule her will power every time. However, she also knew that she couldn't let her son be abused or mistreated like she had been as a child. So with every ounce of motherly love that she possessed, she made a decision that she knew she had to execute right then before she changed her mind. She looked into her baby's eyes and knew what she had to do. She packed Rob Jr.'s things in a bag, put him in the car and drove him over to his father's house. She knew that Rob Sr. was a great dad and loved the baby dearly. And if he knew what was going on at Tia's house, he would probably kill Joey and her.

When Tia pulled up to Rob Sr.'s apartment in the Midway Housing Projects, a neighborhood just as run down as hers, she sat in the car for ten minutes and cried because she hated what she was about to do although she knew that he would be better off with his dad. Once she pulled herself together, she unloaded her baby, gathered his things and walked up the small flight of stairs to Apartment 5b. When she got to the door, she saw a big yellow eviction notice stuck to it. Her heart dropped and she started to turn around and walk back to the car because how was Rob Sr. going to take care of their baby if he didn't have a place to live. But when she looked into her baby's eyes she knew that he still would be better off with his dad.

She knocked on the door and when Rob Sr. answered in his pajamas, she assumed that he'd still been asleep. She knew that he worked third shift at the Textile Mill Sunday through Thursday and would be suspicious as to why she was dropping Rob Jr. off on a Tuesday.

"Tia, wassup?" He asked groggily.

"Uh, Rob. I, I can't keep Rob Jr. anymore and he needs to stay here with you for a while until I get myself together. "

Still half sleep and discombobulated, Rob. Sr. replied, "What? What are you talking about Tia? You know I can't keep him during the week because I work third shift and I don't have anyone to keep him."

"Listen Rob, I'm sorry but this is the only way. I will come by from time to time and bring you money and pampers but I can't keep him anymore. I have to go."

Beginning to realize what was happening, Rob Sr. retorted, "What the fuck is going on Tia? Are you smoking that shit again? Is that nigga you wit mistreating you or my son? You know I don't play that shit. What the fuck is up?" He then noticed the eviction notice on his door. He snatched off, read it and let out a few choice curse words.

"Rob, I gotta go." Tia replied. And with that, she kissed Rob Jr. on the cheek, hugged him and put him down. She ran quickly to the car as Rob Sr. yelled behind her. She quickly jumped in the car and sped off. When she was gone far enough to where she knew he couldn't get to her, she pulled into a shopping center and cried her heart out.

Meanwhile Rob Sr. continued to stand in the doorway bewildered by what had just happened. He loved his son but he knew damn well he wasn't in a financial place to take care of him alone. He picked his son up, carried him into the house, sat down on the floor and stared at the wall. "What the hell am I going to do?" He thought to himself. He sat there wanting to cry but he knew that he couldn't because there was not time for that. He had to come up with a plan.

The first thing he worked on was trying to find someone who could watch his son while he went to work. His neighbor Lakresha, whom he knew was in love with him agreed to keep his son for the night. The next thing he did was gather everything he could find in the house that he could pawn so that he could get up enough money to hold off his landlord until he could get the money to pay all of his rent. He was able to come up with 250.00 which his Landlord took begrudgingly. He threatened Rob Sr. that he'd better have his money by the end of next week or he was out.

When Rob Sr. finally did get to work that night he was tired as hell but felt good that he had made some small accomplishments. The next two days went smoothly until his boss told him that it was mandatory that he work Friday and Saturday night due to it being time to do inventory. Normally, he would have jumped at the idea because he definitely needed the overtime but he knew that he couldn't continue to let Lakresha keep Rob Jr. She had started making sexual advances towards him because in her mind since he didn't have any money to pay her with, then she should be paid in *"some form of way"* and getting him into bed was just what the doctor ordered. But Rob knew that if he started that then he would have to keep it up. And Lakresha; with her cigarette burnt lips, waywardly blonde hair and excessively obese body definitely couldn't make his eyebrow rise, much less his penis, so he tried hard to find someone else. Unsuccessful, he went back to Lakresha but by then she was uninterested. He tried to call in sick but his boss told him that if he didn't show up for mandatory inventory then he would lose his job. Panicked, the only thing that Rob Sr. knew to do was to take Rob Jr. with him to work, leave him in the car and give him some Benadryl praying that he would sleep through the night until he got off from work at 6:30 the next morning. He knew that he could come out to the car every so often and check on him to make sure he was ok. It worked that Thursday night but Friday night didn't go as smoothly. Rob Jr. woke up in the middle of the night alone and panicked by his unfamiliarity with his surroundings. A female security guard doing her nightly rounds heard the child screaming at the top of his lungs and called DSS.

Carolyn Black

"Damn Jermaine, you betta give it to me daddy. Ohhh, awww, smack that booty baby and smack it hard." I cooed as Jermaine hit it from the back during one of our late night sex sessions. But just as he was in midstroke, my work cell phone began to ring.

"Don't answer it baby. It's the weekend." Jermaine said as he continued to pump my insides out.

"I have to baby; I'm on call this weekend. Duty calls." I replied as I reached for the phone.

"Carolyn, this is Debbie." The intake operator replied. "Listen, I'm sorry to bother you so late but we've got a kid that was left in the car at the Textile mill on Stokesdale Lane. The security guard heard the little boy crying and called us and the police. Apparently, the dad didn't have a baby sitter and bought him to work. "

"Ok Debbie. I'm on my way." I sighed as I climbed out of Jermaine's warm arms and went to take a quick shower. Luckily the hotel that Jermaine and I were at was not too far from the mill so it only took me about fifteen minutes to get there. When I got there, the man I assumed to be the dad was sitting in his car with a look of anguish on his face as he talked to the police officer. As I approached the scene, the officer met me before I got to the dad. "Hi, my name is Officer Burroughs."

"Carolyn Black, Fosterberg County Department of Social Services." I replied as I shook his hand.

"Dad's name is Robert Thomas, Sr. Apparently he didn't have a babysitter and brought the child to work for the past few days. The problem is that dad told me that he has been giving the child Benadryl to keep him sleep and of course you know anything could have happened."I shook my head in agreement and headed over to talk to the dad.

"Hello, my name is Carolyn Black and I'm with the Fosterberg County Department of Social Services." I said as I reached my hand out. He appeared dazed as he accepted my

handshake with a very weak one of his own. Then as if the realization of who I was (DSS) and why I was there (to possibly take his kid) began to sink in, the look of anguish was replaced with one that was insidious or ominous even. I, sensing a potential attack began to slowly but stealthily back up. I could see the rage building up within him as his eyes became wide and fury filled.
In a demon possessed voice that foreshadowed calamity, he said,

"Bitch you ain't taking my boy. I don't give a fuck what you say; I will kill your ass before I let you take my boy." And with that he jumped out of the car and lunged at me.

Ready for his attack, my self-defense skills immediately kicked in. So by the time he got to me, his ass was on the ground before I even realized what had happened. I sat on his back and restrained his hands behind his neck so that he couldn't move. The police officer, who was a day late and a dollar short, ran over to us and handcuffed him. As he got the man up off the ground, the officer looked at me in awe. I winked at him and turned around as I heard what I assumed to be the baby crying. He was a precious little boy with big black eyes and shiny black curls to match. He was in the backseat of the police car and had seen everything. I ran over to the car, picked the boy up and tried to comfort him. I walked away from the police car and turned the baby in the opposite direction so that he couldn't see his daddy being loaded up into the car. Finally, he calmed down and I took him to the hospital to get examined to ensure that he was ok. Once I was given the ok, I called around to find a temporary placement for the child; took him there and went home. It was about 5:00 in the morning when I arrived home but I was still revved up so in order to calm myself down, I drank a glass of wine and smoked a joint that Jermaine had given me. Once I was calm, I went to sleep because I knew that I would have an early morning.

When I got up, I made a visit to the county jail to talk with the child's father. I knew that he had acted out of emotions and impulse so I forgave his insurrection. He was sitting in the waiting room with a police guard standing by, dressed in an orange jumpsuit looking as if he hadn't slept a wink all night. I am a pretty good judge of character being that I've been in this field for so long and I could look at the man and tell that he wasn't criminally negligent but more so a regular man who was doing his best to take care of his son.

"Hey Mr. Thomas. I know the way we met last night was due to undesirable circumstances but I need you to know that I'm not here to harm you or imprudently take your child from you. Again my name is Carolyn Black and I'm a social worker. I came to get your side of the story about why your son was left alone in the car and why you have been giving him Benadryl." I said as empathetically and *cautiously* as I could.

He smiled a weak smile and said, "Damn, you strong as hell. I would apologize for attacking you but you kicked my ass last night so that's all the apology you get from me." I smiled warmly at him and we both let out a little laugh which helped us both to relax a little.

"Where's my baby?" He asked as tears began to well up in his eyes.

"He's ok." I replied. I assured him that the baby was safe in a temporary placement and that he would get him back once I got to the bottom of things and was certain that no intentional abuse or neglect had occurred. When I said the words "temporary placement" he broke down. He sobbed uncontrollably for what seemed forever. I let him cry because I knew that this man was at the end of his road and was not only crying for his son but for everything else that was going wrong in his life. Once he had collected himself, it's like the flood gates opened. He started with telling me how his baby mama had dropped his son off and he didn't know where she was at or how to find her. He also told me about the eviction notice and his frisky neighbor who wouldn't keep the baby without him giving her the goods. I asked him why he hadn't come to DSS to ask for help and he bluntly replied that, "Y'all don't help men. This system is set up for female single parents not men. I know because I been there before to get help when I needed help with my rent and the lady looked at me like I was trash." I knew exactly what he was talking about and silently agreed with him.

After talking to him and carefully assessing his character; I was sure that he was a good dad. I wanted to give him his baby back but I still had to go through the proper procedures and do a little investigating before I could let the child come home. I asked several more questions and obtained the necessary information that I needed from him. We concluded our meeting and I was able to persuade the magistrate (who I'd had a couple of rolls in the hay with) to drop the charges and let him go home.

When I got back to the office on Monday; in hopes of finding the baby's mother, I looked up the baby's name in the system because I was sure that he was receiving some type of service. Once I found him, his mother's name and address also popped up so I decided to see if I could catch up with her. But first I went by Rob Sr.'s house to conduct a safety assessment. I needed to see what kind of living conditions the child would be residing in and if there was food, water and electricity. Once the house check was thoroughly done to my pleasing, I informed Rob Sr. that I had to investigate a few more things before I could comfortably return his son to his home.

I left and made my way to the address I had for Rob Jr.'s mother. When I arrived at her apartment no one was there so I went to talk to the landlord who informed me that Tia Barksdale had moved out a couple of days ago. The landlord informed me that Tia had been dating some drug dealer named Joey that lived in Franklin Park. The landlord, whom to my advantage was very nosy, gave me a piece of mail that he had found in the apartment after the couple had moved out. I wrote the address down and made my way to Franklin Park. Franklin Park was a nicer apartment complex but I still made sure that my switchblade was secure within my bra because I didn't know what I was walking into. When I knocked on the door, a very pretty but rough around the edges, young woman who looked to be about 23 opened the door.

"Hello. My name is Carolyn Black. Does Tia Barksdale reside here?" I asked politely.

"Who are you? And why you looking for Tia?" The girl

replied.

"Well I can't release that information unless Tia gives me permission to do so."

She looked at me for a second and then replied, "I'm Tia Barksdale. What do you want with me and how did you find me?" I showed her my badge and assured her that she wasn't in any trouble but that I just needed to talk to her about her son. She looked a little spooked and asked, "Is my son ok? Oh my God I knew that I shouldn't have left him. I knew it."

"Is it ok if I come in so we can talk more privately?" I asked. The apartment although sparsely furnished, was spotless clean. I asked if I could sit and revisited her previous statement about dropping her son off at his dad's.

"So tell me what makes you feel like you shouldn't have dropped your son off at Mr. Thomas' house Ms. Barksdale?"

As tears streamed down her face she replied, "Because I saw that eviction notice on the door and I knew Rob was gonna have a hard time taking care of him. What happened? Did he loose the apartment and have to give my son up?"

"Uh, no ma'am, your son is ok. I just have some questions for you. So when you said you dropped your son off to him that must have been a terribly hard thing to do for you. Can you tell me about that?" She dropped her head and began telling me about how she was addicted to crack and had dropped the boy off because she didn't want him to grow up like that. She also told me that she had been in love with Rob Sr. because he was such a good man but that it had been her that had ruined everything because she had been wild and had wanted to be free. She talked about how good of a dad Rob Sr. was and how she had felt bad about leaving the baby there knowing that Rob Sr. was struggling and didn't have any family as a means of support.

Once I was sure that she was telling the truth, I told her what happened. She cried harder and told me that she now felt even guiltier about leaving the child. But I empathized with her and praised her for being so selfless as to do what was best for her son. I informed her that she had done the right thing and that this was one of the greatest acts of love that I had ever witnessed. She asked what she could do to help and I simply told her that I wanted her to come to social services and switch everything from her name i.e. her section 8 agreement, Medicaid, food stamps and whatever other services that she was getting for Rob Jr. into Rob Sr.'s name. She didn't put up a fight and agreed to come with me so that we could get as much done as we could within the remaining timeframe that we had left for the day. I also requested a copy of the baby's birth certificate and social security number to give to Rob Sr. On our way to DSS she talked about her own childhood and how she had been in and out of foster care due to her own mother being on drugs. She just kept talking about how proud she was that she hadn't followed in her mother's footsteps as far as having a dead beat dad for her child.

When we arrived at DSS, I linked her with the right people and contacted Rob Sr. to come down to the office and meet with us. When he got there and saw Tia sitting there, he became livid but calmed himself down because he was more concerned about the welfare of their son. When she told him about her drug use and crack binges, they both broke down and held each other. We discussed the plan and services that would be put in place. Once we got everything squared away, I told them both that the foster parent that had Rob Jr. would be arriving soon with Rob Jr. so that he could return home with his father. Tia began to get fidgety and said that although she loved her son, she didn't want to see him because she didn't want to be in and out of his life. She said that she didn't want to see him until she was clean. I secretly was proud of her and wished that some of our other parents were as selfless.

I gave her some information on some local drug treatment agencies and told her that she could contact me any time if she needed me. She took the information and told me that she would catch the bus home so Rob Sr. and I could finish up. I gave him daycare vouchers, the remaining portion of his rent and told him that he soon would be able to be on section 8 since he already resided in a section 8 area. He was ecstatic but when he saw the foster parent carrying his son come through the door, he became oblivious to everything else we'd discussed. He grabbed Rob Jr. and squeezed him so hard that I thought he would break the little guy's back. I congratulated Rob Sr. and gave him my card in the event that he needed anything further.

My heart was overjoyed because I rarely had happy endings in these types of situations. I was given the boost of contentment that kept me doing this job. I walked up the stairs with a smile on my face and went to my office to grab my briefcase where I ran into Val. She told me that since I had basically worked all weekend, she would give me the next two days off. I gladly accepted. On my way to my car I saw Jenetta's ugly ass leaning up against the wall talking to Mario. By the way she was leaning; I could tell that she was trying to entice him. I laughed to myself because by the way *he* was standing; I could tell that he could care less. Knowing that she was jealous because Mario and I were much cooler than they were, I decided to mess with her. I hated her guts and would do anything to cause her grief so I sashayed over to Mario and spoke to him, therefore diverging what little bit of attention he was giving her to me.

"What's up Mario?" How's it going?" I asked as I batted my eyes and put my arm around his shoulder.

"What's up Carolyn? I heard about that case you just closed and I give you mad props because not too many men have the opportunity to get assistance like these women do. I appreciate you looking out for him."

"Thanks. Just doing my job." I replied not even acknowledging Jenetta's ass.

"Let's go to Jar Bar and have a drink. Want to?" He asked looking only at me, completely aware of the game I was playing with Jenetta. He knew because he and I joked about Jenetta on a regular basis. We'd created secret little games and hand gestures that we used when we were around her; or other people, to talk about them. Mario knew she had the hots for him and because neither of us really liked Jenetta, we had a little fun torturing her from time to time. There were plenty of times when we would have conversations around her and act like we didn't even see her. We thought she would catch on after a while and back off but nothing has worked thus far.

And right on cue as if she was reading my thoughts, she opened up her stupid mouth and said, "I think that would be great. I'm starving." But this time she looked at me and winked her eye.

"Wow," I thought to myself. "The dummy finally caught on. It's about time." I wanted to punch that heifer in her in the face but I had to applaud her effort. Mario and I looked at each other and shared a silent giggle with our eyes. We both knew her routine and weren't surprised at her self invite.

"Let me go grab my briefcase and we can head out." Mario said as he headed back into the building, leaving me alone with the Wicked Witch of the West.

"Listen Carolyn, I know what you're trying to do and I think you need to back off." Jenetta sneered in her weak attempt to "warn" me. I laughed right in the heifer's face because there was no way in hell that she was going to intimidate me.

"And what is that Jenetta? What am I trying to do?" I asked with a sarcastic giggle.

"You know I'm trying to pursue Mario and you are doing everything in your power to sabotage that for me." She said as seriously as she could. However it only made me laugh even harder.

"Girl, bye. Me and Mario are just friends. Plus, contrary to your beliefs, um, he doesn't want you. I don't see how you haven't caught on to that yet. And the sad thing for you is that no matter how hard you're trifling ass *pursues* Mario, he will never want you. Now he may give you a courtesy screw or should I say, a sympathy screw, but that's it. He likes classy women, not fake, conniving little tricks like you."I snapped. That shut her up.

"Slam dunk in your face!" I thought to myself as she stood there speechless with her mouth hanging open.

At a loss for words, she yelled "Screw you!" and stormed off right as Mario was coming back to rejoin us. I burst out laughing all over again and looped my arm in Mario's as we headed to the car.

"What was that all about?" He asked through giggles.

"Well let's just say, the heifer decided that she didn't want to go after all." I replied.

"Welp, screw her! Let's go get drunk." Mario said as he opened the car door for me. So we headed to the Jar Bar, one of the most popular bars in Fosterberg County. All the "professionals" went there because they had great food, great drink specials and some of the best music one could ask for. Plus there was an air of loyalty and camaraderie amongst us because we could all get drunk and party without scrutiny or judgment. But most importantly, we all followed a "no snitching" code.

Tonight happened to be Reggae night, so it was beyond packed. I was excited because I knew that I didn't have to go to work for two days. So I knew I was going to dance my butt off and get wasted. I was filled with glee as Mario and I were seated at our table. He ordered drinks while I went to the bathroom to freshen up. On my way out, I ran right into my oldest sister, Olivia. All the color drained from my face and the excitement slowly left my body as I sighed and sucked my teeth. I thought to myself, "Here we go." She sneered her nose and looked at me like I was a poopy diaper. I, knowing that she was about to rain on my parade, had every intention of looking at her and walking on by but she on the other hand, had other plans.

"Hello Carolyn." She said in her usual patronizing voice.

"Olivia." I responded in my usual "kiss my ass" voice. Again I attempted to keep walking but it seemed as if she was bound and determined to ruin my night. She stood with her hand on her hips wearing a bright red v-neck top and a pair of wide legged jeans. She actually looked beautiful with her chocolate brown, smooth skin and wavy, jet black hair that fell down past her shoulders. She had my mom's petite frame whereas my other sister and I shared the hour glass figures from my dad's side of the family.

"I assume you're coming to Sylvia's birthday party next week." She stated without any emotion or desire for me to really come.

"Of course I'll be there. She's my sister." I replied with false modesty covered in sarcasm.

"Humph." She responded. "So, who's *that* man? Which one is he?" She asked with a devious snicker, referring to Mario who was watching from our table.

"None of your damn business." I said as poise and coolly as I could, not wanting to let her get to me. Her mouth flew open as if she was about to retort, but I walked off before she could get any further words out. She stood there watching me, defeated. As I returned to the table, Mario must have noticed the distressed look that I had on my face.

"What's wrong? What did she say to you?" He asked.

"Nothing. Forget about it. Let's just party." I replied.

"Nah Cee. What's up? Tell me." So in between shots of vodka, I told him about my sister and filled him in on the history of our relationship.

"Screw her. She's a hater Carolyn. Matter of fact, you're right, let's go party." He stood up, took my hand and we headed to the dance floor.

That next weekend I begrudgingly attended my sister Sylvia's birthday cookout at our parent's house per my mother's request. When I arrived, my sister's and their husbands were there as well as their kids. There were also several other family members there, all of whom were way older than me or way younger than me. The cousins within our age group were always late which meant I was going to be sitting around by myself looking crazy until they got there. Mom and dad were all over the place either cooking or entertaining so I couldn't waste extra time talking to them. And of course I was the only single person there within my age group because even my little brother had some raggedy looking hag with him. A hag by which I ended up hanging out with because my brother was helping my dad with getting the food together. Under different circumstances I probably would have never hung out with her but my choices were limited and I felt sorry for her because she was also sitting alone. So out of desperation, I clung to her as she also clung to me. I; however, was able to conceal my desperation because I was her man's big sister and that gave me some clout. I had the upper hand with her and I could act as if I was just checking her out on my brother's behalf. But my sisters, whose sole goal was to ridicule or embarrass me, saw right through me. They knew that isolation was quickly approaching for me and they knew I wasn't going to hang out with them. Therefore when they saw me engaging in an extended conversation with the girl, they knew I was grasping for straws. I saw them out of the corner of my eye plotting and whispering amongst themselves as they looked in our direction.

The girl, whose name was Tina, was sitting beside me at a table my parents had set up in the back yard for the party. She actually was pretty cool even though her appearance said otherwise. She definitely wasn't the prettiest thing I'd ever seen and she was dressed as if she didn't get out that much. She wore a long curly wig that was on its last leg and a tight black dress that was so short her coo coo was at risk of being on display. She wore a pair of red patent leather chunk heels that I hadn't seen since the 90's and hoped to never see again. Her legs were hairy and she was skinny with big green eyes that popped out their sockets. She had three gold teeth and wore too much makeup. Her face had noticeably large pores and her self painted, long purple finger nails were chipped and broken. But I also noticed that she had large lips and watermelon breasts, thus the reasoning behind my brother's sole purpose for having her. Nevertheless, she liked to trip out and shoot the shit like me. Plus she did a good job of being a diversion for me. I knew she wasn't going to be around long anyway so I really didn't care that I was using her. My brother changed girls like girls changed their panties so her days were numbered.

Although I was using Tina, I still showed her respect unlike my persnickety sisters. They weren't at all shy about what they thought about Tina because they'd let her know early with their condescending looks and blatantly rude comments. They made it apparent that they looked at her as being gutter trash and nothing more. They also knew how our little brother was; therefore, they were downright nasty to her. But she kept her cool and took their abuse like a soldier.

As Tina and I were chatting, I saw them walking towards us. I took a deep breath, thinking to myself, "Here we go."

"So I see you're scraping the bottom of the barrel again huh, Carolyn. Mommy and daddy are too busy hosting the party so they can't *tend* to you and now you've opted to hang out with the trash.

"How...modest of you." My sister Sylvia said as she and my sister Olivia shared a snicker. They were dressed like two Stepford wives in long color coordinated sun dresses and they played the role of two mean girls who thrived off tearing other's down. I didn't know how to respond because if I went off then that would add fuel to the fire and if I didn't say anything then I would be letting them run over me. I was so angry that I wanted to beat the hell out of them but I knew that would only make things worse. I felt like I was no longer tough, kick ass Carolyn Black because I had allowed them to turn me into Carolyn Blah. No one could get under my skin the way they could. But I had a trick up my sleeve. I knew that Sylvia's husband had had an affair and I knew who the woman was that he'd had the affair with. I knew her because her roommate had gotten a CPS report and I was assigned the case. Both of them were prostitutes but they were more "high class" than the ones walking the streets.

During one of my visits to their home I ran into Sylvia's husband, Carl as he was walking out the door, zipping up his pants. When he saw me, he froze as if he'd seen a ghost. And when he regained his ability to speak, he begged me frantically not to tell Sylvia. I just stood there wearing my poker face. I let him assume that I was angry when in actuality I was beaming at the fact that I now had some real ammunition to use against my sister. Although I had no plans of telling Sylvia anything, I damn sure wasn't going to let him know that. I figured that out of anticipation and guilt, he'd hang his own self and tell her; which he did. She of course swept everything under the rug and continued walking around as if her tarnished and obviously lackluster marriage was perfect and happy. I; however knew otherwise. She never said anything to me about the affair and she knew that I knew, yet her cold treatment never ceased. I guess she thought that I was so oppressed by her treachery that I would be too submissive to bring it up. Little did she know I was just waiting for the right time to coolly slide it in and there was no time like the present.

"Trash, huh? Well I bet she's a lot better than the trash that I saw *Carl* hanging out with or should I say, having an affair with. Matter of fact, you might want to go get tested for STD's. I heard she used to be a prostitute." I replied sarcastically, returning the same malicious snicker that she and Olivia had given me. Sylvia's mouth dropped to the ground and Olivia looked like she was in shock because she was totally unaware of Carl's tryst. Sylvia however, quickly regained her composure and just like a quintessential mean girl, she cleaned up her mess and turned the tables back on me.

"You high yella bitch. How dare you tell vicious lies like that on my husband because you're unhappy and desperate. And the gall of you to say in front of...outsiders." She said calmly as she looked in Tina's direction with disgust on her face; totally dismissing the fact that I'd revealed her secret. But I wasn't going to let her get off that easily.

"You dirt brown heifa, don't be mad at me because you're ass is so stuck up and boring that your man had to seek out a prostitute for some excitement."

"Carolyn you are pathetic! You hide behind your career because you have nothing else. You walk around here on your high horse but you ain't shit. So many men have run through you I should call you a tunnel and you still ain't found one that wants to stay. You're in your mid 30's and you're not even close to having someone that even *thinks* you're special enough to spend the rest of his life with." She said in a tone so icy that even Tina was moved. Her words were like little knives jabbing me because I partly believed that what she said was true. Nevertheless, what I was saying was true as well and I still wasn't backing down.

"So because your husband didn't physically leave you makes you think that you're special? Your husband is cheating on you and as long as he stays physically but leaves mentally, you feel special because he's there? Well I tell you what Sylvia, I'd rather be alone and desperate than in a fake ass marriage where my husband solicits prostitutes instead of screwing me. And let me tell you something dear sister, all those supposed men that have run through me; I guarantee that I could *physically* have them again if I wanted to. Then they can go home and I don't *mentally* have to deal with them anymore until they want some of this good Juicy again. And by the way, maybe I can give you some lessons one day so you can learn how to *sexually* please your husband." The heifer stood there quiet with her mouth slightly ajar because she didn't have a comeback. "Boom!" I thought to myself. "And this battle goes to...Carolyn Black."

"Whatever Carolyn, you're still a whore! Come on Olivia, let's go. Leave these two losers over here to feed off each other's misery." She then turned to Tina and said, "My brother's going to screw you and drop you back off in the projects. So don't get comfortable. Oh and by the way, Carolyn's only using you because she has no one else to talk. Ta Ta." She said and turned to walk off.

"Y'all are some evil ass bitches. I haven't done anything to you and that's the last time y'all are going to talk to me like that." Tina said, I guess feeding off my energy, gaining some courage.

"Who in the hell are you calling a bitch you dirty looking, poorly dressed skank." Olivia responded, finally getting in on the action.

"Bitch, I'm talking to you." Tina replied, putting emphasis on the word bitch.

"Little girl you don't want none. You better stop while you're ahead." Sylvia said in a serious tone. Now if there was one thing I knew about my sisters, I knew they could fight. They were snobby and prissy but my father had taught them just like he'd taught me. In my mind I was thinking to myself, "Boo, you really don't want any." But Tina kept talking so I quickly intervened.

"Tina, listen you need to stay out of this because this is between me and my sisters. I apologize for saying this but they're right about my brother. I'm not trying to throw salt on his game but it is what it is. You probably won't be around long. And yes I was talking to you because I didn't have anyone else to talk to. Plus you looked like you needed me as much as I needed you. So just chill out because you won't have to deal with any of us for much longer."I said as gently as I could but not wanting to spare her from the truth.

"I get it Carolyn but they have been disrespecting me since I got here and I'm tired of it and I want an apology."She said, as her tone rose.

"You need to calm down and lower your tone. And we ain't apologizing for shit, this is *our* parent's home and nothing you have to say matters. Now I suggest that you get your raggedy ass out of here before you get *put* out of here." My sister Sylvia hissed, trying to repress the hood that threatened to come out of her. Tina, on the other hand; who missed the cue, wasn't able to restrain herself from letting the hood come out of her any longer. Hell, she *was* hood and she was proud of it. But more than anything I think she was tired of my sister's abuse. Plus, I think she assumed that I had her back and I definitely think that she underestimated my sister. Before I knew it, she mugged Sylvia and the next thing I know, she was getting up off the ground with a bloody nose. Tina was a fighter though and didn't give up. She landed a couple good hits to my sister's face but they weren't enough to save her. Sylvia wore her out while Olivia stood on the sidelines watching, making sure that things didn't get out of control. I knew Olivia wasn't going to jump in because she knew Sylvia could hold her own.

Soon, everybody at the cookout came running over to see what was going on. I crept back and blended in with the crowd. I didn't want any parts of this disaster. I figured the two of them could clean this mess up together. Meanwhile I watched as my pristine, proper sister, turned into gansta boo. My parents were mortified, my little brother was angry and for once my sisters were the center of negative attention. I felt sorry for Tina because she got her ass kicked, but to me she was a causality of me and my sisters' ongoing war. A war that had been going on for the majority of our lives. But I didn't get too excited about my victory because I knew that Sylvia would just retaliate and the repercussions would be swift and painful.

Case #32483 Don't Wanna Let You Go

"Fosterberg Department of Social Services, this is Carolyn Black speaking."

"Um, yes, Ms. Black I want to make a report please. I know this is crazy for me to be making this report on my own son but I love my grandbabies and he's really messing them up."

"Ma'am, tell me what's going on? Who is your son and what is he doing to the children?" I asked.

"Well, to be honest ma'am, he's beating the shit out of his wife and my ten year old granddaughter; who is the oldest, is jumping in it. I love my boy but I didn't raise him like that and I'm afraid one of them babies is gonna get hurt. I keep trying to get them to let the kids come live with me but he won't have it and that dumb wife of his keeps going right back to him. I'm at my wits end and I don't know what else to do."

"Have the police been contacted ma'am?"

"Well, I've called em' two or three times, the kids call and so does his wife but soon as he gets outta jail, she goes and picks his crazy ass up. She says *she loves him*." The lady said, apparently mimicking the voice of the wife. She had a very thick southern drawl and she slurred her words as if she'd been drinking.

"Well ma'am I appreciate you calling me and making this report. Give me the address and I will go by and see what's going on."

"His name is Quincy Campbell and they live at 2122 Freedman Street. The kid's names are Felicity, Marty and Quincy Junior. Felicity is ten, Marty is three and Que is one. "

"Thank you ma'am. Someone will go out to the home soon as possible."

"No, I need someone to come now. You don't understand. He just beat the hell out of her and Felicity got her arm broke in the midst of it trying to protect her mama. He left the house and they came here. They are safe right now 'cause they here with me but when that fool comes back, I know her dumb ass will go back to him. Please. You gotta send someone now." She pleaded.

"Ma'am, I'm going to call the police just in case he does return and we will get someone out there as soon as possible."

She released an impatient sigh and reluctantly accepted. I hung up the phone and called the sheriff's department and talked with them about what was going on. I told them I would meet them out there. I then picked up the phone and called Mario, but he was already out so I reluctantly called Zian which in my opinion was basically me going out by myself. But I had to follow protocol so I dialed her extension. She immediately came over and we headed out.

On the way there I briefed her on what was going on and how important it was for her to keep her eyes open and be alert at all times. I told her that she needed to stay by the door and make sure that she frequently looked out the window.

"I gotcha Carolyn. " She replied looking at me with an "I really don't gotcha" look.

"Girl don't be going in here looking all scary and stuff either because if you do, you're gonna lose all your power and make the family feel uncomfortable. Put your poker face on."

"Ok. I will. But listen, I've got some good news." She squealed with excitement.

"What?"

"I'm getting married and I really want all of y'all to come." She said as she waved her beautiful diamond in my face.

"Awwww. I'm so happy for you Zian. You know I will be there as will everybody else. When is the big day?"

"Three weeks from tomorrow." She replied glowing like the sunshine. She was such a cute girl, light-skinned, dark brown eyes, a round apple face, and a china doll bob.

"Damn girl, you ain't wasting no time are you? When did you get engaged?"

"Well I been engaged for about a year but he was just recently able to afford the ring so I didn't want to say anything until I had a ring to show off."

"Oh, ok. Awesome. You've already sent out your invitations right?"

"Yeah, but I was going to hand deliver y'all's though so I can save on postage costs."

"I know that's right." I said as we pulled into the driveway of a gray and white trailer that looked as if its best days were gone. The sheriff department was already there and standing in the yard talking to a petite black woman with a thick mass of bushy hair. I greeted the sheriff and turned towards the young woman. The whole right side of her pecan brown face was black and blue and her eye was damn near closed. As we approached them, an older white lady with a polka dot house dress came out the front door. I wondered to myself who she was because it was apparent that the woman with the black eye was Mrs. Campbell.

"Mrs. Campbell? Hi, my name is Carolyn Black with the Fosterberg County Department of Social Services."

"Damn, Geraldine! You called CPS on me? What the fuck is wrong with you?" Mrs. Campbell yelled.

"Well, you dumb bitch, I'm tired of you and that good for nothing son of mine putting my grandkids in the midst of y'all's bullshit." The old woman retorted.

"That's our business. Not yours you old drunk. And who are you? You can't stay sober long enough to know what's going on anyway. You need to stay the fuck out of our business!" As I stood there watching this exchange between the two women, I was at a loss for words. I couldn't believe they were out in the middle of the yard in front of me and the police squawking like two hens.

"My grandchildren are my business. If you and my son wanna kill each other that's fine with me but them babies shouldn't have to deal with that mess."

"Um, excuse me ladies. I'm sorry to have to interject but I need to talk with you Mrs. Campbell about the welfare of these children and what we can do to help you out."

"Bitch, there ain't a damned thing you can do to help us out. This old bat called you for nothing. I have my kids and their lives under control. I don't need no help from the likes of you or nobody else." I took a step back because my initial reaction was to slap the taste out of this rude heifer's mouth. I took a deep breath and looked over at Zian who looked petrified. "Welp, no help from her ass." I thought to myself. I regained my composure and approached the situation from a different angle.

"Mrs. Campbell, let's try this again. I work for CPS and if you're children are at risk of any kind of harm then my job is to ensure their safety. If you and your husband are fighting in front of them or around them, then that puts them at risk, *therefore* if you don't make some kind of changes in this situation then your children will be coming with me. Do I make myself clear?" I stated bluntly.

She balled up her fists like she was going to hit me and I automatically stepped into my fighter's stance. This silly bitch was really crazy but then I thought differently about it. This woman was probably defensive because her children were probably all she had and although her husband beat on her, she was probably adamant about not letting anybody else hurt her. In a way I sympathized with her so I calmed down and allowed my professionalism take over.

"You ain't taking my kids. I don't care what you say." She hissed.

"No ma'am. I don't want to take your kids. Kids are better off with their natural parents." I paused then said, "Listen Mrs. Campbell, I'm not here to cause you any harm. I'm just doing my job. I believe you are probably a good mother but do you really want your children to see their mother whom they love dearly getting hurt or fighting with their father? I don't know if you've looked in the mirror or not but if you haven't then you need to. No child wants to see their mother going through this Mrs. Campbell. Studies have shown that children who are exposed to domestic violence become a part of a cycle. Either they become an abuser or the victim and I know that you don't want your daughter being beat on by a man or your son hitting a woman."

She looked down at the ground. I guess she thought about it because I saw tears welling up in her eyes. I was hoping that I hit a nerve with her.

"Now Mrs. Campbell, I know that your daughter is getting involved in these fights with you and your husband. She's only ten years old and although she's doing what any child would do to protect her mother, that's not her responsibility and it's very dangerous. So please..." I took her hand in mine. "Let me help you."

"I know but I love Quincy. We been together since I was fifteen years old. I don't know what happened that made him like this but he loves his kids and he's a good daddy. You don't know him. He's not a bad guy, he just gets upset sometimes and his anger gets a little out of control. And it's not like he just beats on me, we fight each other." My heart sunk as I listened to her excuses. I knew that eventually, I was gonna end up having to take these children into custody. I knew she wasn't going to leave him. I put my head down and then looked over at Zian who was shaking her head. Just then, a black Toyota Tundra pulled up into the driveway. Inside was a very handsome young man who looked like he was a marine. He had very low cut blonde hair, sky blue eyes and a nicely chiseled body. He jumped out of the truck and made his way over to where we were all standing. The rage that I saw in his eyes made the hairs on my arms stand up. I actually was afraid.

"Jalisha, what the hell is going on here? Mom, what are these people doing here?" The man I presumed to be Quincy, asked as he looked between his mother and wife.

Neither responded. Jalisha looked scared to death and

Geraldine wore a look of disgust. I, on the other hand, prepared for the worst because I had no idea of what he was going to do or if he was going to try to hurt us. I had my trusty razor blade hidden in my bra and had no reserves about cutting his ass up if he tried to hurt me or Zian. But because the sheriff was now standing beside all of us, I felt relieved because I knew he could handle it.

"Answer me bitch! Who are these people and why are they here?" He screamed, getting into Jalisha's face in an attempt to intimidate her.

"Sir, I think you need to calm down or I'm gonna have to arrest you." The sheriff replied while easing his hand over his tool belt. Quincy looked around, took a deep breath and calmed himself down. I assumed that like most male batterers, he was a punk when challenged by a man.

"I apologize for my rudeness. I'm just confused about why you people are here and what's going on." He responded. Not falling for his new "calm" mood, I put a little space in between us and introduced myself.

"Hello Mr. Campbell, my name is Carolyn Black and I work for the Fosterberg Department of Social Services. I received a report about you and your wife fighting in front of the children and I'm here to investigate. And your wife's blackened eyes and swollen face makes it apparent that the report had some validity to it. Now, I haven't met with your children yet, but is it true that your daughter has a broken arm?"

"A broken arm?" The wife and husband asked in unison. They both then turned and looked at Geraldine who put her hand on her hip and looked right back at them like she didn't care if she'd lied or not.

"Look, I lied but I don't give a damn. Them kids get put in the middle of y'all's crap on a daily basis and sooner or later one of em's gonna get hurt. Especially Felicity cause both y'all pieces of trash know that she jumps in the middle of y'all's fights."

"Mom, what the hell is wrong with you? Me and Jalisha's problems are our problems and it's none of your damn business. Did you ever listen to me and Andy when we tried to get you to leave dad when he was beating the shit out of you?" He screamed with his finger in his mother's face.

"Did I get in your freaking business when you was passed out drunk or so high on cocaine that you couldn't be a mother to me? Huh bitch? Was I? All I did was love you regardless of the shit you did to me and Andy. Now I'm all messed up in the head and Andy is dead. And who's fault is it you good for nothing, alcoholic old bag? Yours!"

At the conclusion of his rant, Quincy was so enraged that his face was red, the veins in his head and neck were popping out and he was foaming at the mouth. Each of us witnessing this scene between mother and son were so taken aback that we were all speechless; including the sheriff. Geraldine on the other hand looked like she was ready for war. She reared her arm back and smacked Quincy with every bit of strength that she had in her body. And surprisingly, this big tough young man cowered back like he was a five year old little boy. By this time, the sheriff and I intervened. I took Geraldine with me and Quincy went with the sheriff. He took him for a ride just to get him away from the situation. I felt as if we had been in the midst of a family therapy session. However, at that point I didn't care. All the chaos had almost made me forget why I was there and that was for the children and their mother's safety. I had Zian's scary ass to go into the house and get the children while the sheriff and I deescalated the situation. Only the ten year old came out of the house because the two younger kids were in daycare. And she was a heavenly angel with long light brown tendrils of hair that cascaded around her small pecan brown face.

My heart went out to her because the expression on her face definitely didn't match her angelic appearance. She had an overpowering sadness about her and her eyes had lost their youthful sparkle. I was glad her father was gone because I could talk to the little girl without any drama. I introduced myself to her and told her why I was there. She shook my hand and told me that her name was Felicity. Although she was nervous, she was a brave little girl. She wasn't afraid to tell us about how her father beat on her mother and how she would pick things up and hit him so that he would leave her mother alone. I asked her if he'd ever hit her and she said that he'd hit her once or twice but admitted that it was because she had done something really bad. The child also admitted that he was a good father to her and her siblings but she couldn't deal with the way that he treated her mother. Felicity told us that she had sprained her ankle and had been smashed into the wall while trying to protect her mother from her father. As the child talked, I glanced over at Jalisha who was visibly shaken by the things her child was saying. I strongly hoped that hearing these things would compel her to leave.

After talking with Felicity, I turned to Jalisha and asked her what she was going to do to address the situation. In an assertive but empathetic tone I told her that I would not be leaving today until I was sure that her children were going to be in a safe environment. I told her that she had two options; either the children had to leave the home or Quincy had to leave the home. I informed her that we would set up batterer's counseling for Quincy and family counseling for the family. I also told her that Quincy would be allowed to have supervised visits with the children until he was cleared to have unsupervised visits. Jalisha looked away and didn't respond. I gave her time to think because I knew this was hard for her. She loved her children and she loved her husband; however, her children had to come first.

"Mrs. Campbell, what would you like to do?" I asked gently.

"I don't know. You're putting me between a rock and a hard place Ms. Black. He doesn't mean to hurt me. You just heard what he went through as a child. He's just doing what he knows to do. I can't just leave him because he doesn't know any better." She responded quietly.

"Mrs. Campbell, if it was just you and him then you could do whatever you wanted to do. However, when you involve children, you involve me and if you choose to keep him in the home, then the children will be removed. We are willing to help Quincy get the help he needs but right now you are enabling him and keeping him from getting better. You're not holding him accountable and he will beat you until one or both of you die if you don't put his feet to the fire".

Felicity; who was looking at her mother in disbelief, dropped her head. Finally, she began to speak.

"Mom, I'm sick and tired of this. Why mom? Why do you let him do this to you? I can't take it no more. Y'all fight almost every day. You never come to visit me at school and you always miss everything because you're always beat up. My brothers cry all the time and you're never able to do anything with us because you're always sick or hurt. And daddy…." Her voice went down to a whisper. "Daddy never even apologizes for what he does to you. He comes home and you go in the bedroom with him and then y'all are all made up until the next time."

She became silent for a second then looked at her mother and said, "Mommy, I love you but if you don't leave him for good I don't wanna live with you no more." And with that being said, the little girl got up and went back into her grandmother's house. I looked at Jalisha and asked her what she was going to do. I informed her that time was up and she had to make a decision. She began sobbing uncontrollably and Geraldine who had also been standing there throughout the discussion, looked at her with disgust.

"Damnit Jalisha, leave his sorry ass. Don't, don't be like me and put a man before your kids. Quincy was right. The way he turned out is all my fault. It's not you that he's angry at, it's me. All them years that his good for nothing daddy beat on me I never left him and social services wasn't the way they are now, neither was the police. A man could beat on a woman back then and nobody really said nothing unless they nearly killed ya. He needs help Jalisha and you can't change him."

"My son Andy..." Geraldine paused as if she had a lump in her throat. The hard shell that she'd been wearing the entire time began to crack. She swallowed hard and then continued.
"My son Andy, he, he killed himself because he couldn't deal with it. His daddy was beating me and I was using every drug I could get my hands on just so I could deal with the pain. When Andy killed

himself, I finally got the strength to leave that son of a bitch but I had to lose my son in the mean time. I thought that because Quincy was only eight years old he would be ok but he ain't Jalisha. He ain't. He's his daddy made over and I can't hardly stand to look at my own son. Please Jalisha, please! You are a good girl with a future. Leave and leave now." Geraldine pleaded.

"Jalisha, I know you love him but Geraldine's right, you can't change him. He needs help and in the mean time you've got three babies to think about and we've got to put together a plan for them." I reiterated.

"Ok, ok." She whispered. "I'll press charges and get a restraining order, but I just can't keep his kids from him. They love him."

"Don't worry Jalisha; we'll work all of that out." Zian replied. I almost broke my neck as I whipped it around in Zian's direction. I was surprised that she'd even said anything because I'd barely heard her speak the entire time. Hell I'd almost forgotten that she was even there. I was impressed. The heifer could talk.

When the sheriff returned with Quincy, Jalisha told him that she was going to press charges and take out a restraining order. The officer cuffed Quincy and took him downtown. I was so proud of her. We all hugged her and headed out. When Zian and I returned to the office, we immediately started working on getting services in place for the family. Geraldine had agreed to allow Quincy to stay with her and she also agreed to serve as a liaison between the two parents when it came time for Quincy to see the kids.

Three Weeks Later

"Oh my gosh Carolyn. I can't believe that Zian is getting married. I'm so happy for her. Have you ever met her fiancé?" Val asked in her normally giddy manner as me, Mario, her and her husband Maurice rode to the wedding.

"No I haven't met him but every since she told us she was getting married she hasn't stopped talking about him. His name is

Avery or something like that." I responded.

"Do you know what he does?" Mario asked like I was Inspector Gadget and knew all of the girl's business. I assumed that was because Zian and I had been spending so much time together trying to help the Campbell family get situated. She'd been very passionate about the case and had really helped the family get linked with a lot of different services. I was really proud of her and I felt that she needed to be more on the treatment side of DSS versus the investigative, CPS part.

"I think she said he has some kind of contracting job that sends him all over the state doing different kinds of projects. Sounds to me like he has some money." I laughed.

"Well let's hope so." Val replied.

We arrived at the wedding venue and took our seats. Of course we were on CP time and barely got there before the ceremony started. As the groom and groomsman walked down the aisle all the color drained from my face. My heart stopped and I could barely breathe. I would have passed out if it wouldn't have caused a scene. Val; who was sitting beside me, saw my reaction and asked what was wrong. I could barely speak but in a forced whisper I replied, "Val, that's Jermaine. The groom, the groom is Jermaine. Oh my God! That's Jermaine."

"Carolyn you dumb ass." I thought to myself. "Why didn't you investigate his ass more?" He was the only man out of my collection of toys that I didn't know anything about and as dumb as I thought he was, he'd outsmarted me because the fool's name wasn't even Jermaine. Normally I wouldn't have given a rat's ass but I really liked Zian and didn't want to hurt her. She was so young and naïve but more than anything she was a really sweet girl who thought she was marrying a decent man. I was about to shit myself, but Val on the other hand was getting a big kick out of the drama. She loved drama because her life was so damn boring.

"What you gonna do Ms. Black?" Val asked sarcastically in between giggles. I didn't find the shit amusing at all. Nevertheless the damage was done and I could only shake my head and hope that Zian would never find out.

"I don't know Val but I can't go to that damn reception because we won't be able to avoid them.

"Carolyn, we are two and a half hours from home, where are we gonna go? Just pretend that you don't know him." She said with a smirk. I wanted to slap her because the heifer was really enjoying this. I knew she wasn't going to be of any help and I couldn't tell Mario so I was trapped like a rat. But I knew that I would eventually figure out a way to avoid them.

The ceremony was beautiful of course and Zian looked simply beautiful in her long, lace A-line gown with a sweet heart neckline. She was breathtaking but I felt sick on my stomach because I felt like I was betraying her. Yes I made it my business to screw other women's husbands but I never crossed the boundary with people I knew or considered to be a friend. Even though I couldn't stand Jenetta's ass, I still had enough respect for her not to sleep with her man; if she ever got one.

Speaking of Jenetta, Zian had placed her at the same table with us which meant I had to be tortured with her presence throughout the entire reception. She hadn't ridden down with us so I assumed she'd driven there by herself. I felt a little bad because she could have easily gotten in the car with us but Val's husband had driven therefore I didn't have anything to do with it. Although I couldn't stand her, I still got a kick out of her being around because I loved to antagonize her.

Once we were seated, I had to think fast about what to do. I made the decision to pretend like I wasn't feeling well. I'd noticed a somewhat secluded lobby area in the rear portion of the venue on our way to the reception hall. I figured that it would be the perfect place for me to "hideout" until the reception was over. I told Val; who was laughing at me so hard that she almost pissed her pants, to cover for me. I wanted to punch her in the face but what could I say because I knew that sooner or later my trysts were going catch up with me.

When I reached my destination, I sat down on the couch and leaned back with my eyes closed. Although I wasn't physically sick, my mental state made me feel nauseous. I was so pissed at myself for slipping on my pimping. "How could I have let this dum dum get one over on me?" I thought to myself. I knew that he had somebody but my indifference and lack of concern for knowing anything about him had come back to bite me in the ass. I really didn't know how I was going to get out of this one especially since I worked with Zian and would eventually run into him.

I stayed in my secret spot for as long as my bladder would allow. Finally I couldn't take it anymore and got up to go to the bathroom. What a mistake that was because Zian and Jermaine were standing in the hallway talking as I walked around the corner. The pee that was almost running out of my eyes dried up and the eyes that used to sit inside my sockets popped out. I tried to turn and go another way but it was too late. They both saw me so there was no avoiding them. Jermaine, I mean Avery, looked like he was feeling the same way that I was once he realized who I was. Whereas my eyes were bulging out of my head, his were frozen in a state of disbelief. Zian; being her normal, doe-doe bird self, was completely oblivious to the shock waves igniting between Jermaine, I mean Avery and I. She was overcome with giddiness and was beyond excited to introduce me to her new "husband."

"Carolyn! Carolyn! Come here! I've been looking for you all afternoon so I could introduce you to my husband, Avery. Where have you been girl?" She asked, glowing. My heart broke into a million pieces as I stood there looking at a man who had screwed me in every way possible.

"Zian you look beautiful. I, I um, I wasn't feeling too well and I had to go somewhere so I could lay down for a sec." I said as I tried by all means to avoid Jermaine, I mean Avery's face.

"Well, I hope you feel better girl. Meet my husband Avery. Avery this is my co-worker Carolyn, Carolyn this is my husband, Avery." She said with a squeal of happiness. He weakly shook my hand as we exchanged halfhearted hellos.

"Well Zian I have to go to the restroom. I'm really happy for you." I said genuinely as hugged her.

"You've got to come back in for the bouquet toss, ok?"

"Ok." I said as I turned to head to the bathroom.

"Nice to meet you Jermaine." I said weakly, attempting to be courteous. But when I realized that I had called him, Jermaine, I quickly corrected myself and scurried into the bathroom. I almost died. My heart was beating out of my chest and once I began to pee, I swear I peed for about an hour.

When I finally got myself together, I rejoined the party. I felt relieved that I had gotten that situation over with because now I could go and have a good time. As I approached our assigned table, I noticed that Mario was talking to Jenetta. I laughed a little wicked laugh to myself as I plotted. "Welp, I ain't gonna be the only tortured soul here today." I thought to myself. I figured, "What the heck. I might as well ruin Jenetta's day too." But first, I needed a stiff drink so I summoned a waiter to bring me a glass of wine. As soon as I got it, I gulped it down like it was water.

"Damn girl. You needed that drink didn't you?" Jenetta said in a tone that oozed with sarcasm. I ignored her ignorance and did something that I knew would hurt her worse.

"Mario lets go dance. Want to?" I asked as I gave her a malicious look, unbeknownst to Mario. She gave me the evilest look in the world but as I took Mario's hand and headed towards the dance floor, I looked at her and winked.

The Campbells

Jalisha knew that she was going to lose her children, but her love and loyalty to Quincy held her captive. He'd rescued her from her drug addicted mother and a pimp that was in the midst of putting her out on the streets. She owed Quincy and she knew that if she loved him enough and got him some help then he would change. She got up early that morning and cooked breakfast for the kids and made sure they were safely off to school and daycare. When she dropped Felicity off, she hugged her a little longer and kissed her a little harder than she usually did. Felicity looked at her mother with confusion because of the unusual display of affection. But she brushed if off, thinking that her mom was finally starting to relax from the fear that she'd sustained at the hands of her father.

Felicity had been so happy the past three weeks since her father had been gone. She'd finally been able to get a good night of sleep. The house had been so peaceful without the sound of her mother's screams, her father's vulgar words and things breaking. Her mother; however, had seemed uneasy and on the edge the whole time. Felicity thought that maybe her mother hadn't gotten used to the peaceful environment yet. But something was different with her mom today. She looked calmer and more relaxed. She looked almost happy with a look of contentment that Felicity didn't recognize. She took a deep breath because now maybe her mother was beginning to see how good life could be without her father being there. But the more Felicity examined her mother's face, the eerier she began to feel. The look in her mother's eyes appeared to be familiar but she allowed the new feeling of peaceful bliss that she was experiencing to make her oblivious to her mother's awkward behavior therefore she ignored it.

With about fifteen minutes of the school day remaining, the school secretary contacted Felicity's teacher over the intercom and informed her that Felicity would be a bus rider today. Felicity wondered what was going on but again ignored that familiar pang of anxiety that threatened to trump down her new found happiness. In the past, most of the time when she had had to ride the bus home it was because her mother was too badly beaten up to pick her up from school. But Felicity thought to herself that this time something had to be different because her mom had promised not to let her father come back because the nice lady from DSS had warned her that she would lose Felicity and her brothers if she did.

On the bus ride home, no matter how hard she tried to ignore her feelings and focus on her newfound peace, Felicity began to get nervous and her hands started to shake. She began sweating and her heart was beating out of control. She didn't understand why because she was safe now and her father was gone. She forced herself to think about how good things were for her now and fought off the stress that was trying to overcome her. However, her feelings won the battle and her mind was overwhelmed with fear. She tried her best to be hopeful and prayed that her mother had been doing something that had kept her from picking her up from school. However when the bus pulled up at her house, her father's truck sat in the driveway. The anxiety that had knotted up in her stomach began to churn and she almost threw up. Fear and anger began to consume her as she braced herself for what she was about to walk into. Walking down the aisle of the bus to the door was like walking the green mile. She took her time because she knew that once she got off the bus, her short lived world of happiness would be over. When she opened the front door of her house, the lamp was lying on the floor broken; there was a hole in the wall and her mother sitting on the couch smoking a cigarette. Her hair was in a disarray, her leg was shaking profusely and she had a fresh black eye and busted lip. Felicity's one year old brother, who was sitting on his mother's lap, was screaming at the top of his lungs and her three year old brother was sitting beside their mother trying to console her.

Felicity stood in the doorway and took the whole scene in. She didn't see her father, but his presence was palpable. Her mother intentionally avoided Felicity's stare because her shame wouldn't allow her to acknowledge Felicity's disappointment. As she looked around the room, realizing that she had walked back into hell, hands shook uncontrollably and the vomit that had threatened to spew out of her churning stomach while she was on the bus, made its way out onto the floor. Once she'd finished vomiting, her mind shut down on her. She dropped her backpack on the floor and walked towards her bedroom as if she were a zombie.

"Felicity, Felicity, come give your daddy a hug. I've missed you. Oh my God Felicity, you threw up all over the floor. Are you ok? Well aren't you gonna clean it up? Damnit Felicity, don't you hear me talking to you?"

No, she didn't because the sound of her father's voice sounded as if it were merely a whisper in the wind, blowing up against a tree. It sounded so far away that Felicity didn't know if she'd really heard him or not. She just kept walking as if she was in trance or a state of sub consciousness that would only allow her to think about one thing; regaining her sense of peace. She walked straight into her room and locked the door. She opened her closet door and found her pink and purple stripped jump rope out. She tied the jump rope in a tight knot around her neck, stood on her desk and tied the other end to a bar near the ceiling that went from one wall to the other. It was as if she was having an out of body experience; watching herself doing what she was doing without being able to control or stop herself. She no longer had control of her movements or her mind because her central nervous system's commencement of fight or flight was in fifth gear. The pain and anxiety, the fear and disappointment, her mother's betrayal and disregard for her and her brothers and her overwhelming anger was unbearable. She knew that as long as she was alive, those feelings and emotions would never subside. She knew that that gut wrenching feeling that she woke up to almost every day would be there waiting for her every morning. She knew that her hands would always shake; she knew that the food she ate would never be an ally providing her with nutrients because it would always be an antagonist, disrupting her already upset stomach. Her short ten years of life had been a tumultuous whirlwind that had continued to get worse and worse as she grew older and became more aware of what was going on. She knew that she had no control over her parents and the hell that they subjected her to. But for this one precious moment, she finally had the opportunity to choose whether or not she would continue to endure it. She closed her eyes and thought about the three weeks of peace that she'd had; the peace that she knew that she would never see again as long as her weak mother kept going back to her father. She knew that Geraldine, DSS nor anyone else could save her and she would never feel that short lived peace again because even if her mom did leave her dad, she now knew that it would only be a mirage, a tease, or a cruel joke. The thought of never having that peace again was too much for her to bear so she smiled her last smile and jumped off the desk.

Carolyn Black

"Fosterberg County DSS, this is Carolyn." I said as I answered the phone. It was Monday afternoon and I looked at the clock with excitement because I knew that in one more hour I would be heading to the hotel to meet Dewayne. I got wet just thinking about what kind of gifts he would have for me. I knew he'd been pissed at me after our last encounter but I didn't care because I knew that he would be back.

"Hello?" I repeated because I didn't hear anything on the other end besides something that sounded like heavy breathing. I thought it may have been Dewayne calling to get me hot and bothered before I came by. But the heavy breathing turned into sobs and I knew for certain that it wasn't Dewayne.

"Hello? Who is this?"

"Ms., huh, huh, Ms. Black. This is, huh, huh, Geraldine Campbell." Geraldine said, sounding as if she had to force herself to speak. My body stiffened and my heart began to beat rapidly, as I could only imagine what was going on. I just knew that she was going to tell me that Quincy had killed Jalisha.

"Ms. Campbell, what's wrong?" I asked. Geraldine let out a loud, almost deafening sob.

"Ms. Black, Felicity tried to kill herself today. We're at the hospital and they don't think she's going to make it." My heart stopped, as did everything else in the room. For a second, I think I stopped breathing and tears swelled in my eyes.

Regaining my composure, I replied, "Geraldine I'm on my way." I hung up the phone and quickly began to gather my things. As I rushed towards the door, I almost knocked Val and Mario over. They stopped me and through my compromised ability to breath, I quickly briefed them on what was going on. I really was in no shape to drive so Mario drove us all to the hospital.

When we arrived; Geraldine, Jalisha, Quincy and the smaller children were all sitting in the waiting room. All of their faces were red and swollen from crying. Jalisha had another black eye and I shook my head as I pondered how this woman could continue to endure such abuse.

When Geraldine saw us coming in, she jumped up to meet us. She told us that Quincy had found Felicity hanging in her bedroom after she'd come home from school. Geraldine broke down and buried her head in my chest as she cried. I did the best I could to console the woman but I wanted to break down myself. The thought of that precious little girl being in so much pain that she'd resorted to hanging herself broke my heart. Quincy also came over to me and in the most humble and genuine tone I'd ever heard from him, he said to me, "Ms. Black I swear before God if my baby lives I will never come around them again unless they want me to come around. I love my kids dearly and I love Jalisha too but I never realized how much this situation has affected my babies. Now I see how my brother felt. He couldn't deal with it but I on the other hand internalized it and became a walking time bomb. I will do anything. I will go to the psychiatrist, doctor, therapist or anybody to get help. I just need my baby to be ok." He said, breaking down into sobs.

I believed him but at that point I had no sympathy for him or Jalisha who was sitting in the chair staring off into space. Just then the doctor walked out to talk with the family. The fact that his face was a white as a ghost let me know that he didn't have good news.

"Um, I'm sorry to say this but uh, Felicity didn't make it." The doctor stated as soothingly as possible. Jalisha passed out and Geraldine let out a blood curdling scream. Quincy simply sat on the ground Indian style, put his thumb in his mouth and started rocking. Val, Mario and I stood in the waiting room in disbelief. None of us had ever experienced anything like this before. I fought back tears as I said a silent prayer and hoped that that precious little girl was finally at peace.

Case #32484 My Angel

"Here Angel, take this and it will make it easier for you."

"No mom. Please. I don't wanna do this again. I don't like doing this."

"Look Angel, you got to pay your way around here. Now you know school will be starting soon and you know you need some school clothes. I'm barely working and I can't afford to go out and buy you new clothes. Plus you got to eat, have somewhere to sleep and have lights. That stuff ain't free. Now do it and shut your mouth."

Angel looked down at the thin white lines of cocaine neatly lined out on the small mirror her mother was holding. She felt nauseous and afraid. Tears began to roll down her face as she thought about how bad she wanted to run and hide so that she wouldn't have to snort the cocaine. She thought about her beloved dead grandmother whom she'd lived with prior to coming to stay with her mother. She knew that if her grandmother could see the things that she was doing now, she would be rolling over in her grave. But she had no choice because she was now at the mercy of her mother; who was a drug addict and a self made pimp.

Initially, she'd been happy about finally getting to be with her mother whom she'd dreamed about as a child. She'd always imagined that her mother would be loving and kind, just like her grandmother had been. But after living with her mother for less than a year, she had been in for a rude awakening. Once her mother had seen the gold mine that she had in her beautiful, nicely built daughter; Angel had gone from being an innocent 13 year old girl to a 14 year old mother made stripper, doing "strip parties" for anyone who would pay her mother to see her dance.

The "parties" were always held in the basement of their house because the basement had a fully stocked bar and a newly installed stripper pole. There was also a small bedroom off to the side and sometimes for the right price; Angel would have to do more than just dance. To mollify things; her mother always gave her cocaine and vodka. She told Angel that the substances would "make things easier" and make her oblivious to the immoral acts in which she engaged. But nevertheless, although the drugs made her feel anesthetized, Angel was always fully aware of what was going on. And once she had come down off her "high" she always felt dirty and worthless. She never saw any of the actual money that *she* made. However; her mother, being the *pimp* that she was, always provided Angel with the things that she needed. Sometimes her mother would even buy extravagant things like expensive jewelry or designer purses. And although everything that Angel had was name brand, she still felt cheap and shameful.

"Girl if you don't hurry up and do this line, I'ma smack you into the middle of next week." Her mother snapped. She looked at her mother; who was unfazed by the tears that were falling from her eyes in disbelief and reluctantly snorted one of the lines. Her mother then handed her a glass of vodka, which she gulped down since she'd gotten used to the taste. She actually liked drinking vodka because it didn't make her feel the way the coke did. Either way, she would zone out and do what she had to do to please her mother.

"Now hurry up and go get dressed! They'll be here in a minute." Her mother said as she basically pushed Angel off into the bedroom. Angel turned and slowly walked into the small room in the basement where she began putting on her naughty school girl outfit and the massive amount of makeup that she hoped would mask how she was really feeling. As she was getting dressed she heard the doorbell ring and her mother's oversized body climbing the stairs to answer the door. She also heard her mother say, "Down this way boys, the show's about to start in a minute." She took a deep breath and closed her eyes. She sat on the edge of the bed with a strong desire to sob as loudly as her lungs would allow, however she knew that she couldn't mess up her makeup. She stood up and looked at herself in the mirror. She didn't even recognize herself anymore. She was a 14 year old girl living the life of a grown woman who was a prostitute. Her grandmother had always told her how pretty she was but she'd warned her about men and how they could take her beauty and transform it into a depleted harshness if she allowed them to take advantage of it. The thought of her grandmother began to incline her to run for her life; however as the cocaine and vodka began to kick in, she pushed the thoughts of morality out of her mind. She shook herself back into reality as she strapped up her 4 inch black stripper shoes and tapped on the door to alert her mother that she was ready. Once the music began to play, she left the innocent child at the door and transformed into the provocative woman that her mother had taught her to be. She sashayed seductively towards the pole and began to dance.

Marsha watched her daughter as she gave individual lap dances and maneuvered around the pole. She took a sniff of cocaine and put her head back against the wall. She thought about how weird it was for her to be so jealous of her own child. Angel was as beautiful on the inside as she was on the outside. She had a beautiful figure and an onion shaped backside that Marsha knew would drive men wild. When she looked in the mirror at herself, she saw a fat, brutish looking woman who *used* to be beautiful. However, her beauty had gotten her into trouble. When she was around Angel's age, she had gotten raped by her preacher while spending the night with his daughter but when she told her parents they didn't believe her. So on every Sunday, Wednesday and any other given day of the week, she was forced to look at him standing before her preaching about the goodness of God, singing hymns and condemning sin. A man, who she'd once trusted, admired and looked up to. A man, who was very well respected and a dear friend to her parents. An attentive man, who had complimented her smile, her pretty hair and "cute little button nose". A man who had lured her away from the slumber party taking place in his daughter's room so he could talk to her about "something important". A man who made her feel relaxed and calm as he rattled off about random things that were anything but important. A man who coaxed her into lying on the ottoman in his office with her eyes closed. A man who started out massaging her feet and then gradually worked his way up until his stubby fingers found their way inside her. A man who put his hand over her mouth and then raped her. She remembered feeling nasty and ashamed.

There were times during church services or other church functions when she would catch him looking at her with that hungry look in his eyes. Finally, when his advances started going beyond stares she stopped going to church. Her parents tried everything from beating her, grounding her and telling her that she was going to Hell; to try and force her to go. But nothing they did, no matter how extreme, could make her budge. Things got so bad that they eventually kicked her out. She went from house to house staying with friends until she ran up on a random stranger that introduced her to the escort business. Her beauty made her a lot of money but it also made her a lot of enemies. She got hooked on cocaine and her expensive drug habit took her from being a high class call girl to a back alley hooker. From there her life did a downward spiral. Cocaine became too expensive so she started using Meth. She was raped several more times by some of her tricks and taken advantage of by her smoking buddies. It got to the point whereby she became so desensitized to sex that she didn't care when, where or with whom she did it, as long as she was paid something or at least given a hit. But when she met Angel's father, things were different with him. He was an older white man who came in, helped her get clean and provided her with stability. He gave her the world and as a result, she fell in love with him. As time progressed he became mean and controlling. He started having rough and almost sadistic sex with her. She thought he loved her so she did what he wanted. But after he'd started beating her she couldn't deal with it anymore and left him. Once she was safe and living with some of her friends, she cut all her hair off and vowed to never touch men again. At the time she hadn't realized that she was pregnant with Angel. When she gave birth to Angel and saw how beautiful she was and how much she resembled her father, she couldn't bear to look at her. She tried for a long time to raise Angel. But one night when Angel was about two months old, she just wouldn't stop crying. She became so overcome with rage that she found herself getting ready to choke Angel. It had scared her so bad that she handed Angel over to her mother and didn't look back. At times the guilt overwhelmed her and she would go and visit Angel, but she would never stay long because it was too painful. Now that she had Angel living with her, she had no inkling about what it meant to be a mother because it had been fourteen years since she'd tried it. Her heart was so ossified by her refusal to feel any type of emotions that even her mother's intuition had dissipated. All she knew to do was protect Angel by exposing her to the conniving and wicked ways of men early. She started teaching Angel about how her beauty was a curse and how it made her a target. She didn't want Angel to be naive and caught off guard like she had been. So she made sure that Angel knew not to trust men; even those that said or pretended like they loved her. She was training Angel to know that her vagina was a gold mine and as long as she knew how to use it right, it could work for her and not against her. After each "show" or "party", she sat Angel down, showed her *their* earnings and critiqued Angel's performance. The more money Angel made, the more extravagant the reward was. She knew that what she was doing to Angel was cruel but she didn't want Angel to be dumb like she had been and give her hot box away for chump change. If they were going to take it anyway, then she wanted Angel to have something to show for it. And at least with her monitoring Angel's every move, *she* could control the situation and not some stranger who was gonna lie to her and use her. Once she was sure that Angel knew the ropes and was in control, then she would back off and watch from a distance.

As she stood surveying the room, basically making sure that

the guys didn't get too rough, Kiam; the young man who had requested the party as a gift for his homeboy and who was also her drug dealer, came over to her. He asked for some Hennessy and handed her four hundred dollars and two grams of cocaine. She knew that the two grams of coke was a request for the "special treatment." She accepted but told him that if they were all going to get the "special treatment" then it would be 200.00 dollars per half hour, per guy. He accepted and gave her two hundred extra dollars in the event that they "went over the time limit". He then gave each of his boys a glass of Hennessy and passed around a blunt as they sat back and enjoyed the show. None of them knew that Angel was her daughter and assumed that she was just a girl that Marsha was "managing."

After Angel finished dancing, Marsha motioned for her daughter to come over to the bar. She poured her another glass of vodka and prepared two more lines of coke for her to snort. As Angel approached and saw what her mother had to offer she stiffened. Although she was still buzzing from her previous "trip to Aspen," she was coherent enough to know that her mother had sold her again and therefore, she was getting ready to have to have sex. At the point, she didn't even argue with her mother. Her previous rendezvous with the coke and vodka had made her horny and indifferent and she knew that she would definitely have to blast off to another world in order to submit to "phase 2" of the party so she did the coke, chugged the vodka and headed to the bedroom. She however, didn't know that she would be entertaining more than one man that night. After she "pleased" one man, she wiped the tears from her eyes and began to get up off the bed. Just then she noticed that another man was coming in. Alarmed, she quickly covered herself and balled up against the headboard of the bed.

"Yo baby, what you scared of? My boy said you give good neck and I paid good money to see for myself." The young man gloated as he walked towards Angel with a ravenous look in his eyes. Knowing that her mother had orchestrated the deal, she closed her eyes, spread her legs and let the young man have his way with her. He was extremely rough and pounded her mercilessly. He treated her as if she was a common whore and relieved himself all over her face. Once he got up to leave, she laid on the bed, paralyzed with shame and humiliation. She took the covers and slowly began wiping her face. Once again she made an attempt to get up and leave the room of iniquity; however she was once again betrayed by her mother who sent yet another man into the room to rob her of another piece of her already depleted innocence. Marsha watched apathetically as three men simultaneously went in to have sex with her daughter. One young man refused to go in therefore she had to give fifty dollars back to Kiam. But it was of no concern to her because she had made 800.00 dollars and had scored some cocaine as well; therefore her job was done.

Two weeks later

Jamar Williams walked into Westwood Middle School with excitement in his heart. Today was the first day of school and it would also be his first day as a student teacher in the 8th grade math class. He had dressed nice and he felt confident about his ability to be the best he could be. He had his black Dooney and Burke briefcase in one hand and his pride in the other. As he walked down the hall, he looked around at the students as they laughed, talked and searched for their new classes. He smiled as he thought about his own teenage years and those that were to come for his two year old daughter. The teacher, Ms. Blackburn, was standing at the door as he entered into his assigned math class to retire his things and get started for the day. She greeted him with a warm welcome and told him where to put his things. He sat his things at his designated desk and returned to stand at the door with Ms. Blackburn. He began having small talk with her about his duties and how things operated at the school. Just as he was about to ask about what not to eat in the cafeteria, he froze and all the color drained from his handsome caramel brown face.

"Mr. Williams, is everything ok? You look like you have just seen a ghost." Shaking it off, he responded that he was ok but had to excuse himself. He wanted to make sure that what he had just seen was actually what he had just seen. He walked down the hall and as he approached the young girl from behind, he knew that he had most definitely seen what he thought he had seen. It was the girl who had stripped at the party that his friends, Richard and Kiam had thrown to celebrate him being awarded the Teaching Fellow Scholarship. She had the body of a twenty year old, but looking at her in the face with no makeup on, he could definitely tell that she was nothing more than a baby. He was sickened at the thought of what he had seen this young girl do. He kicked himself for smoking weed and drinking to the point that he had not noticed that she was a kid. But how could he have known. She looked like a grown woman and the way she'd rode him during his lap dance was extremely equivalent to those that he'd gotten from seasoned strippers at the local strip club. Just thinking about it made him want to throw up. He thought to himself, "What kind of person would allow a child to do those types of things? " He had a daughter of his own and he would have died if someone would have her doing the things that this little girl had done. So as soon as a he got a free moment, he called his boy Richard.

"Yo, Richard man, you not gonna believe this shit dog."

"What's up man? You done ran into some teacher that you used bang out or something?" Richard laughed in anticipation of what his best friend of ten years was about to tell him.

"Hell naw man. I wish that was it. Man you know that girl that stripped for us at that party you and Kiam had for me?"

"Oh hell man, don't tell me *she's* one of the teachers." Richard said as he laughed even harder.

"Hell no man! She's one of the freaking students!" Jamar exclaimed. Richard abruptly stopped laughing and sounded as if he was about to choke.

"What man? A student? What the hell you mean a student? Oh Jesus! I banged her brains out. Oh Lord man! We all going to Hell!"

"Man I know. How you think I feel man, being that I have to look at her every day?"

"What u gonna do man? You think she recognizes you?"

"I don't think she recognized me. I don't know what to do man but we gotta do something. I think I'm gonna call DSS."

"Call DSS? Man are you crazy? She's got to be what, thirteen or fourteen years old? We will all go to jail for that shit man. Especially the way we was smoking weed and drinking and slapping her ass. Not to mention we all had sex with her. Oh my God! I think I'm bought to throw up!"

"Nah man I didn't bang shit! Get that right! I told your ass not to do that with that girl. I knew something wasn't right. But more than anything man, I have a daughter and this girl's parents may not know what's going on. Who knows, that butch looking broad that was with her may have turned her out or anything man. I've made up my mind man. I'm about to be a teacher. I gotta do what's right."

"Jamar man, leave that shit alone. You tell that shit and your teaching career will be over. Don't do it man. Don't do it." Richard pleaded.

"Man, we didn't know that girl was a kid. And I can't wait around until she just happens to recognize me one day and blow the top off all this shit. Look man, I gotta go. I'll call you later. Listen; keep this between me and you until I tell you otherwise aight?"

"Man, I think you need to keep your mouth shut cause I ain't trying to go down for this shit man. But you do what you do man. Holla at me and let me know what's up."

Jamar hung up with Richard, said a quick prayer and headed to the office. He happened to be good friends with the principal's son and had chosen this particular school for that reason. He went into the principal's office and alerted him to what was going on. He made sure to tell the principal that none of the guys knew that the girl was underage. Jamar told the principal that he wanted to call DSS because he didn't know what else to do because the little girl needed help. The principal agreed and immediately called the Fosterberg Department of Social Services.

Carolyn Black

I was having a hell of a day. I was feeling bloated, my head was hurting, I was cramping and my skirt felt like it was about to suffocate me. On this one day in particular, I so wished that I was a man. I was irritable and everybody was getting on my damn nerves. So when I got the call that I needed to head to Westwood Middle School for some report that was being made, I wasn't happy at all. I was so hoping that today would be an easy day where all I had to do was some paperwork, make phone calls and take my black behind home to a blunt and bottle of wine.

I gathered my notebook and brief case and headed to my state car. I took a deep breath, turned on the radio and began listening to "Don't Make Me" by 8 Ball and MJG. That was my "get through my period week" song. When I got to Westwood, I headed straight to the office to check in. I was led into a small room by the secretary where the principal, a young looking man and what appeared to be a student sat in anticipation of my arrival. The student; a young girl, looked distraught and her face was red from crying. I took another deep breath and decided that I needed to talk with the young man first since he had made the report. I asked him to go with me into another room while the principal stayed with the young girl.

"Hello Mr…?"

"Williams. Jamar Williams." He responded as he shook my hand. I looked at him and he appeared to be about 21 or 22 years old. He was very nice looking. Brown skinned, close fade haircut, and the cutest light brown eyes. He had dimples and very pretty teeth. He was about six foot 3 and 195 pounds. Just looking at him made my bloated stomach begin to rumble with passion. In my mind I was thinking to myself, "Good God boy, you just don't know what I would do to your young tender butt!" By his height and the size of his hands and feet I began to imagine how well endowed his package was. Suddenly my hormones began to rage and my body began to make me want to salivate. But I had to jolt myself back into reality and find out what was going on.

"Hello, I'm Carolyn Black, with Fosterberg DSS. I got a report of possible neglect or abuse. Tell me what's going on." As he filled me in on his story about the little girl and how she'd stripped and then had sex with his friends, I was shocked. Not necessarily about what had happened, but more so by him coming forward and making the report regardless of the possibility of getting into major trouble if it was proven that he knew that the girl was underage.

"Ms. Black, I swear that none of us knew. All I know was that my boys were throwing me a party for getting this teaching fellow scholarship and they said they knew some local stripper that threw private parties at her house. When we got there we paid some brute looking broad who led us to the basement for the private party. I don't know who she was but I assumed that she was the girl's pimp or bodyguard or girlfriend. "

"Do you remember any names or where the lady lived?" Jamar sat there and thought for a while. He told me that he had been pretty messed up on the way there and even more messed up after he'd left there, thanks to his boys. But then as he sat contemplating, a light went off in his head. He remembered that he'd recorded the whole thing.

"Ms. Black I have it on my phone. I just remembered that I recorded it." He said as he grabbed his phone out of his pocket and found the video he had recorded that night. As he watched, he appeared very relieved that he had gotten so much footage. He had recorded the girl dancing, the woman giving her a hit of cocaine and liquor as well as the boys going into the room to bang the girl. He wanted to cover his boys back though so he talked to me about the video before he showed it to me.

"Listen Ms. Black, there are some very incriminating things on this video. We were partying and tore up. None of us knew that girl was underage. Please don't penalize my boys for what they did. They don't deserve to get in trouble."

"Well Mr. Williams, if they didn't know then I don't think that we can charge them for ignorance. I just want to know who this woman is." He showed me the tape and as I watched the little girl shake her booty, I couldn't believe it myself. She moved like a pro and had a butt that looked almost as good as mine. Looking into her face, I understood what Jamar was talking about because she had a lot of makeup on and with a body like that; she definitely looked older than fourteen. It was dark and the boys were drinking, therefore I believed Jamar. But what was really disgusting to me was when I saw the woman giving the girl cocaine and liquor before sending her into the room with the boys. I had seen enough and needed to talk to the girl. I asked to keep Jamar's phone so I could show the girl the video and he accepted.

I went back into the room where the girl sat with the principal. She was still crying, therefore I asked the principal to get her a cup of water and leave us alone to talk. Once we were alone, I introduced myself.

"Hi. My name is Carolyn Black and I'm with the department of social services. What's your name?"

"Angel." She whispered. "What a pretty girl" I thought to myself. She was the color of golden wheat and had jet black hair that cascaded down her back. She had a very nice shape and hazel eyes. Sitting in front of me, she looked like a scared little girl, not some girl gone wild, out to make some change. She was dressed like a typical teenage with skinny jeans, a white guess tee shirt and matching air force one tennis shoes. She didn't wear any makeup with the exception of lip gloss.

"Angel do you recognize the young man that was in here earlier?

"No. Not really. But they told me what was going on. I don't remember him." She said with tears streaming down her face.

"Angel, is this something you've done before? And who is the woman in the video?" I asked as I showed her the video. She appeared to be extremely ashamed and embarrassed. She began to cry harder to the point where she began to hyperventilate. I calmed her down and had her to take another drink of water.

"Angel I know this is hard for you but you gotta tell me who this woman is and how long this has been going on."

"She, she, she's my mother and I've been doing these types of things since I moved in with her a year ago, after my grandmother died." She said reluctantly in between sniffles.

"So your grandmother raised you?"

"Yes, since I was a baby."

"How did you feel living with your grandmother?" I asked.

"I loved my granny because she was the best granny in the world but I always wanted my mama. She would come to see me sometimes but her and granny never got along so she didn't come around a lot."

She blew her nose and continued to talk. "I was so sad when my granny died but I was happy to finally be able to live with my mother. I just wanted to make her happy so she would stay this time. I hate what she has me doing but she's mother and I don't want her to get mad and abandon me again."

"Do you have any other family?" I asked.

"No."

My heart dropped because I knew that I was going to have to take this child out her mother's home. The poor child had already lost her grandmother and now she was going to lose her mother as well. I could tell that she loved her mother and although it was an abusive environment, it was familiar and safe to her. It had been my experience that regardless of the maltreatment that children sustained at the hands of their parents, most kids still wanted to remain with them. I prepared myself because I knew that I was probably going to have a fight on my hands but nevertheless, I had to do my job.

"Angel honey, I know you love your mother but I can't let you go back there with her. She's giving you drugs and allowing you to engage in underage drinking. Not to mention, she has turned you into a prostitute. No parent should do that to a child. I'm sorry but I'm going to have to find somewhere else for you to stay ok." I said as gently as I could.

"No, No! I don't wanna go to no foster home. She'll stop, she'll stop. Just talk to her. She'll change. I can't go to a foster home. No, no! I'll die first!" She began screaming.

I took a deep breath and tried to calm her down but my efforts were unsuccessful. Soon, my level of irritability outweighed my professionalism and attempts to be sympathetic. Before I realized what I was doing, I jerked the girl up and got in her face.

"Angel, now look a here damnit, calm down! All that screaming and hollering ain't gonna get you nowhere you hear me. I know you love your mom and I know you feel scared and lost right now but regardless baby you can't go home. What your mother is doing is against the law. Now you can cry, kick and scream all you want to but you've got to go. Now get yourself together and let's go." I said sternly. I hated to be like that but in certain situations I had no choice.

She reluctantly got up and slowly walked with me to the car. I contacted the police and reported what I knew about the situation. I worried about what would happen to the nice young man who made the report but at that point I didn't care. I was sad for the young girl sitting beside me because I knew that she was getting ready to have a very hard time. She loved her mother so much that she would do *anything* for her acceptance. I, on the other hand wanted to kick her mother's teeth out. I called Val and briefed her on what was going on and scheduled an emergency TDM meeting. When we arrived at DSS everyone was in the conference room waiting. Angel and I took a seat while we waited for the police to bring her mother. Angel sat anxiously, biting her nails and shaking her leg. By looking at her I could tell that she was petrified. When her mother walked in, she looked like she would nearly faint so I went and got her some water before we started the meeting. Angel's mother was overweight but she actually had a nice shape although the oversized manly looking clothes that she wore covered up her body. She was cocoa brown with beautiful smooth skin. But she had scars on the right side of her face and her hair was shaved off. She glared at Angel as she sat down across from her.

"What the fuck is going on? She asked, never taking her eyes off Angel, further intimidating her. She showed no fear, empathy or concern for her child; only disgust.

"Intimidate me, you fat heifer." I thought to myself. But I knew that I had to let the group facilitator do her job so I kept quiet. She stated the group rules and informed the woman that she would be asked to leave if she did not abide.

"Do you mutherfuckers think I give a damn about your fucking rules? Just say what you got to say."

"Ms., uh what is your name?" I asked trying to hide my sarcasm and distaste for her. I was starting to lose my patience.

"My name is Marsha."

"Well Marsha, a teacher who happened to be one of the men that you sold your own daughter to during a strip party, made a CPS report. We have everything on video and we saw you giving your daughter drugs and sending her into a room to have sex with more than one man. Not to mention that you had her stripping. Now I'm going to make this short and sweet, do you have any other family members who can take Angel in because she will no longer be residing with you." I said, reciprocating her lack of regard because her nasty mouth and attitude paired with the treatment of her daughter, had rubbed me the wrong way. She looked at me like she wanted to do something to me and I gave her the same look back. Seeing that I wasn't playing, she directed her anger towards Angel.

"Well I didn't want the little bitch anyway. But no I don't have any family she can go to. We was all we had." She said directing that last comment to Angel.

"Well I'm sorry that you're all she had." I blurted out without realizing it. Valerie shot me a "shut the hell up look." Although that was the way I was feeling, I knew my comment was inappropriate in this type of environment. Marsha actually looked like I'd hurt her feelings. I almost felt bad until I thought about her pimping out her 14 year old daughter.

"I'm sorry. I shouldn't have said that ma'am. So what about her father? Do you think he's able to take her?" Marsha uncharacteristically shrunk in her seat. She put her head down and didn't speak for a minute. Then as if the old Marsha had returned, she looked up and said, "Fuck that raggedy mutherfucker. I don't know where he's at. I haven't seen him since he beat the shit out of me 14 years ago. I never looked back. But even if you did find him, he wouldn't treat her no better than I did because hell, he taught me everything I know about the game." She said with a grunt.

"Angel, honey, I'm sorry but we're going to have to have you placed in foster care." Angel; who hadn't really said anything, shifted in her seat and didn't respond. She never even raised her head up to look at me. Marsha, who had been the wicked witch of the west for the entire time, suddenly broke down. To all our amazement, we saw that this woman actually had some humanity.

"Angel, I'm so sorry. This is all my fault but they are right, I don't deserve to be your mother. I've done terrible things to you and haven't been a mother to you for your whole life but I just want to explain. This is not an excuse Angel but I was raped by Pastor Moxley when I was a little younger than you and when I went and told grandma and grandpa, they wouldn't hear of it. I was so hurt because they turned their back on me and now I've done the exact same thing to you. I'm a mess Angel. I've been used and abused and raked over the coals and instead of me embracing you and finding true love through you, I took my pain out on you. Angel go with these people and let them find you a good loving home. One day maybe you'll be able to find it in your heart to forgive me. I love you enough to let you go baby." She got up, kissed Angel on the top of her head and headed back to the officer who put her in cuffs and led her out. Angel sat as if she were in a daze. Zian, who had returned from her honeymoon, took Angel with her to a placement that had been arranged for her. The rest of the team also vacated the room with the exception of Val who ripped me a new butthole because of my attitude and comment. I knew she was serious because she threatened to suspend me if I pulled that again. I apologized and told Val that I was on my period and was in bitch mode.

"I don't give two shits Carolyn. This is all of our lively hoods that you're messing with."

"Ok Val, I understand. I'm sorry. I just kind of lost it. I'm usually very poised but my period plus that woman's attitude and treatment of that child just got to me. My fuse is real short right now." I replied.

"Well get over it." She said sternly and walked out of the

conference room.

"Hmmph, I guess she *told* me." I thought to myself with a giggle. As I was returning to my office my phone chirped, signaling that I had an incoming text message. As I pulled it up, I be damn if it wasn't that sorry ass Jermaine, I mean Avery.

It read: Carolyn, I' m so sorry about you finding out about my getting married this way. I would really like to get together and meet so we can talk about this. I love Zian but she doesn' t satisfy me like you do. I have a serious appetite for your thick ass

I texted him back: Fuck you and never call me again!

He texted: Don' t be like that, you know you love the way my tongue feels in that tight wet twat. We ain' t got to tell nobody

I didn't even text his trifling ass back. I was so disgusted that I almost had a head on collision with Mario while walking to my desk.

"Damn girl. You alright? Where's your mind at?" He asked with a chuckle.

"I'm sorry Mario. Today is just one of them days for me. I'm ready to go home and wash this day off."

"I feel you. Me to. You know what; let's go get a drink when we leave from here. Want to?"

"Hell yeah, as long as you paying." I replied with a sly smile.

"I got you. Let's get outta here."

We went to Jar Bar and sat down for drinks. A local band was there singing an original song that I'd never heard before. Our intentions were to drink and not talk about work but off course that didn't happen. We talked about the crazy situation we had just dealt with and how sad the situation was.

"Man, sometimes I really want to quit this job because some of these people really make me sick and God knows they never cease to amaze me. The only reason I'm still here is because these young black males need a positive role model in their lives and there are so few black men in this profession. I hate what these people do but I guess hurt people hurt people and the cycle just continues." Mario said as he sipped on his glass Hennessy.

"I know. These people do some sadistic, cruel, plain out

crazy shit. Sometimes I wish I could just take these kids home with me." I replied.

"Speaking of kids, when are you gonna have kids of your own Carolyn?" He asked with a giggle because he knew I wasn't really pressed about having kids of my own. I love my life and my freedom. That's one reason why I don't have a real relationship.

"When are *you* gonna have kids Mario?" I asked, placing things back on him.

"When I meet the right woman." He responded as he looked off into space.

"So what is the right woman Mario?" I asked sarcastically as I twirled the straw around in my glass of Grey Goose.

"Well, she's got to be attractive, smart, independent, sexy and down to earth. But I also like a woman who can hold her own and check me on my shit. I hate push over girls. I need a woman who can talk a little bit of shit if you know what I mean." He paused and then looked at me and said, "Actually, I would love to have a woman like you."

I almost choked on my drink but I played it cool like he had made a joke and I responded, "Well, I guess you gonna be in trouble because there's only one Carolyn Black and you can't have her." I laughed and followed up by immediately saying that I had to go to the bathroom. He laughed and shook his head. When I got to the bathroom I took a deep breath and leaned up against the sink.

"What the hell?" I thought. "Where did that come from?" I gave myself a few minutes and prepared to walk back out. Just then my personal cell phone rang.

"Hello."

"Umm, yes, who is this?" A female voice asked.

"Who are you looking for?" I shot back.

"Well, I'm looking for a woman named Carolyn that's been screwing my husband." I almost dropped the phone when I realized that it was Zian on the other end of the phone.

"Shit!" I whispered into the air. I knew I had to play it cool so I hung up the phone praying that she didn't catch my voice. As I headed back to the table, my phone began ringing again. I didn't want it to go to voice mail because I was sure that she would catch my voice so I answered and hung back up. I told Mario that I had an emergency and headed home. I quickly changed my voice mail message to where the automated voice came on and turned my phone off.

The next day at work, we had an early staff meeting so that we could discuss the outcome of the situation with Angel. I could barely look Zian, who appeared to be in another world; in her face because I knew that eventually she was going to find out who I was. But, being a real bitch, I decided that I was going to go ahead and tell her. I had hoped that Jermaine/Avery's punk ass would have just gone on about his life and we could have taken our relationship to the grave but nothing was ever that easy for me. I knew that I was going to have to tell her. I decided to tell her after work so I talked her into having drinks with me at a local sports bar. I didn't want to go to Jar Bar because I wasn't sure how she was going to take things and I didn't want anyone who knew us to witness any confrontations.

When we arrived, we both sat down at the table and ordered drinks and an appetizer.

"Zian, listen, I really need to talk to you about something and I know that you're not going to like it." She smiled and looked at me with that confused Zian look but didn't reply because she appeared to be preoccupied.

"Hold on girl. I've got to make a phone call real quick. I have some unfinished business that I've got to handle real quick. I been calling this whore all day and she won't answer." Oblivious to what she was talking about, I said ok as she made her phone call. Right then my phone also started to ring. Annoyed, I answered it without even looking at the number and when I said "Hello." I heard an echo of my own voice from Zian's phone. She looked at me as if she was in a state of shock and disbelief. And I guess the look of astonishment on my face affirmed that the unfinished business that she had was with me. "Sonofabitch" I thought to myself. If the heifer could have waited ten more minutes to call, neither of us would be sitting here dumbfounded right now.

We continued to stare at each other in silence and disbelief for what seemed like forever. I think it took her a couple of minutes to process what was going on.

"Carolyn, why is the whore who's number I've been calling all day the same as your number? What's going on?" She asked with her usual dim-witted countenance.

"Uh, duh." I thought to myself. "Gosh she's such a ding bat." But nevertheless, I tried to explain myself but I was at a loss for words and I could see her calculating things in her head.

"So are you the Carolyn that's been satisfying my husband in ways that I can't?" She asked as the look of shock became the look of rage.

"Zian, I'm not sleeping with your husband and I never slept with your husband. This is why I brought you here today because I had to tell you what was going on. I never knew that Jermaine, I mean Avery was with you. I didn't even know that he was dating anybody. Hell I didn't even know that his name was Avery. He told me his name was Jermaine and when we were at the wedding that was the first time that I saw you all together and I was in shock. I didn't know how to tell you because I didn't want to ruin your day. You've got to believe me. I would never do anything to hurt you. I'm soooo sorry." I said as genuinely as I could. She appeared to calm down and took a deep breath. She sat there for a while, continuing to process what I said. She then looked at me and smiled, which I thought was very incongruent to the situation. But I soon understood the smile because the next thing I knew I was seeing stars. She hit me so fast that I didn't see it coming. And of course because her ass had been so scary in the past, I had underestimated her. But hell I understood because men can make us do some crazy things. However; just because I understood didn't mean that I was going to let her ass get away with sucker punching me. I jumped out of my seat before she could land another haymaker and grabbed her like she was a client. I put her in a restraint and told her to calm down. By that time, everybody was watching us and out of the corner of my eye, I saw Mario approaching us. "Shit!" I said without meaning to say it out loud.

"Damnit, Mario", I thought to myself. "How is it that he is always in the midst of my drama? What was he even doing here?"

"What the hell is going on over here?" He asked as he got in between me and Zian. Once he separated us, he picked Zian up, who was swinging wildly, and carried her outside. Of course I followed trying to calm her down but the more I said the madder she got.

"Mario, did you know that this trifling ass bitch has been screwing my husband and looking me in my face every day? You whore! I knew something was up when you got missing at my wedding and then you were acting all crazy when you saw us out in the hallway. Bitch I should kill you! How dare you? That's messed up Carolyn. I work side by side with you every day and you been holding this in all this time?" She screamed.

I kept trying to explain the situation to her but she wasn't trying to hear it. Although I was angry and wanted to slap the taste out of mouth and tell her to shut up, I knew that there was no real reason for me to fight with her. I understood her anger and she was truly innocent in this situation. So I turned around to walk away and as I did, I felt a big blob of spit hit the side of my face. At first I was in shock and froze in mid turn. But reality that this heifer had just spit on me sunk in as the slimy, wet substance oozed down the side of my face. In that brief second I forgot who I was and where I was. My ability to retain any fragment of rationality and integrity dissipated with each millimeter that the spit oozed down my face. Mario, who saw the inevitable calamity that was coming, quickly let Zian go and grabbed me. I was so angry that chills were running down my spine. But as Mario hoisted me over his shoulder; which kinda turned me on, I wiped my face with my sleeve, gave Zian a look that made her *wish* I had just punched her in the face and took a deep breath. I counted to ten, I took a deep breath and I counted to ten. I wanted to choke her ass but I just kept repeating in my mind, "She's a baby. She's angry. This is Jermaine/ I mean Avery's fault! She's Zian for goodness sakes! She's a baby. She's angry. This is Jermaine/ I mean Avery's fault! She's Zian for goodness sakes." "Breathe Carolyn, Breathe." I tried to convince myself but as I flopped up and down, over Mario's shoulder, I happened to lift up my head and look at her. She no longer looked like the sweet innocent Zian that I apparently continued to misjudge and underestimate. She had a smirk on her face that spread from North Carolina to Egypt. Then she let out the most taunting little snicker that she could conjure up and mockingly took the outside of her hand and wiped her cheek. And I; on impulse, responded by raising my hand and wiping the side of my face again. At first I felt dumb for responding that way, but as my fingers made contact with the bottom of my chin, they swept across a small spot of spit that had *almost* dried and I lost it. I tried to lung at her but Mario tightened his grip and kept walking.

"Carolyn, stop! You gotta get in your car and go before they call the police. Chill out please." He begged. Zian; who wasn't crazy, retreated to her car and sped off. I, on the other hand was hot. I was embarrassed because everybody, including Mario had witnessed the scene. I was angry because I had let Zian spit on me without smashing her face in and I was mostly angry because Jermaine, I mean Avery, was the only guy I had been dealing with who actually *wasn't* married. He was the one person that I didn't feel any guilt about but he turned out to be my worst choice of all. I was so angry and shaken that Mario left his own car there and drove me around so I could calm down for a minute.

"Carolyn, I know it's none of my business but what the heck is going on?" He asked with genuine concern in his eyes. I didn't really want to talk to him about what had happened but being that he'd witnessed all the drama and had heard Zian's haphazard revelation; I knew that I had to tell him something. So I filled him in on all the information about mine and Jermaine/Avery's relationship, minus the details of our sexual escapades. I insisted that I had no clue about Zian and let him know that I didn't even know that this dude's name was Avery. When I got through telling the story I thought Mario would think that I was a whore, but to my surprise, this dude burst out laughing. I wanted to punch him but the more and more he laughed, I eventually had to join in with him. We laughed for as we drove back to the bar to get his car.

"So what are you going to do Carolyn? How are you and Zian going to work together now? She hates your ass now." He said in between giggles.

"I'm glad your ass is getting kicks out of this Mario. But honestly I don't know what I'm going to do. I hate that things happened like this because I never meant to hurt Zian. That's not my style."

"Well, I can't keep playing referee for you girls because y'all bout took me down earlier." Mario replied just as my phone rang.

"Oh hell, it's Val. Damn! Zian must have called her and told her what was going on. I'm already in trouble for that stuff that went down at the TDM yesterday. Shit! She's probably going to suspend me." I said panicking. In my heart I was praying that she wouldn't suspend me because she had known everything that was going on with Zian, Jermaine/Avery and I. So I took the coward way out and decided not to answer the phone.

"I ain't answering right now Mario. I'll call her back on my way home." I needed a minute to think and prepare before I talked to her.

"Cool with me but I don't think she'll suspend you." He began giggling again. "I'm sorry but this is some *Young and the Restless* shit. I can't help but to laugh. Carolyn you never cease to amaze me." He said in between laughs. I however had gotten serious. Although Mario and I weren't an item, I valued how he viewed me and I didn't want him to see me as being a whore.

"Mario, um, do you think I'm a whore now. I swear I didn't know."

Reciprocating my serious countenance he looked at me and replied, "Carolyn, I've known you for years and I know what kind of woman you are. I would never look at you like that. You are a young woman who's single with no children. You are entitled to do as you please. No, I don't look at you like a whore. You are my friend and that's the way I will always look at you."

Relieved, I smiled at him. I was usually so cautious about my extracurricular activities but this situation made me feel as if I was slipping on my pimping, therefore I knew I had to tighten up.

Once Mario and I parted, I returned Val's call. I wasn't afraid of anyone but in this instance I feared the possibility of losing my job so I was nervous as hell. When Val answered the phone her response to everything that was going on caught me off guard. To my surprise, her response was very similar to that of Mario's. She laughed so hard at me that she could barely speak. At this point in time she was my friend and not my supervisor.

"I told your ass about all these men. That's what your ass gets. Zian told me she beat your ass and sent you home with your tail between your legs." She said in between intervals of laughter. I laughed as well because she knew good and well that Zian could never beat my ass.

"Ok Carolyn, listen on a serious tip, in order to resolve this matter, I need you to take a couple of sick days so I can think about what to do. I think that I'm going to transfer Zian to the foster care department at the Maple Street location. She'll do better with placement anyway. She really isn't cut out for the investigative department. But I don't want her to think I'm punishing her so just go along with things and take a few days off." I was relieved. Not only because I wasn't getting fired but also because I was still PMSing and was glad to have the time off. I gladly accepted and told Val that I would see her on Monday morning. That gave me five days to recuperate. When I arrived home, I took a hot shower, fixed a glass of wine, rolled a blunt and beamed myself up to Scottie.

Case #32485 The Glass House

Mignon looked at the two lines on the pregnancy test and vomited. This was her second pregnancy by her stepfather. The first time; he'd secretly taken her to Charlotte, NC while her mother was away and made her get an abortion. Not that she wanted the baby anyway. He'd been having sex with her since she was fifteen and now she was seventeen. On the outside, everybody thought she lived the perfect life and had the perfect family. Her mother, Judy was a physician's assistant at a prominent doctor's office and her stepfather, Duran was an executive at the local trucking plant. She was a popular basketball star at her high school and had taken the team to three championships, all of which they'd taken home the trophies. She had also won Homecoming Queen and was involved in numerous social clubs. However, behind closed doors, her life was a mess. Her mother secretly had a heroin addiction and her stepfather of course was raping her as often as possible. She tried her best to stay involved with any and everything that would keep her away from the house of Hell but she had to come home at night. And while her mother was somewhere nodding, her stepfather was creeping into her room raping her. Each time felt like the first time and she never got used to it. He had tried to be careful in the past by using condoms but at times he got careless which resulted in what was happening to her now. She was afraid to tell anyone because she didn't know what he would do to her.

He had threatened to kill her before and had even put a gun in her mouth one night while he raped her.

"Mignon, come eat dinner honey." At the sound of her mother's voice, she hurriedly jumped up, washed her face and headed to the dinner table where her mother and stepfather were waiting for her. Had she not known better, she would have thought they were the Cleavers. Her stepfather was sitting at the table reading his paper and her mother hummed as she walked around with her apron tied around her waist, setting the table. Duran greeted Mignon lovingly like she was his own daughter. It never ceased to amaze her how fake her family was. She knew that soon after dinner was done and the kitchen was cleaned, her mother would sneak into the bathroom, do her business and sit staring at the wall until she nodded off. Then once she nodded off, Duran would change from Dr. Jekyll to Mr. Hyde.

Once the table was set, everyone sat down to eat. Duran and her mother talked about their days at work and Mignon talked about her upcoming basketball game. Today was Saturday so she didn't have a game or anywhere in particular to go, so she tried quickly to think of somebody she could go and spend the night with.

"Mom, can I go and spend the night with Grandma Jean because I miss her and I haven't seen her in a while. We hardly ever go over to check on her and I really miss her Sunday dinners." Mignon said trying to butter her mother up. But instead of getting a response from her mother, Duran chimed in and shot those plans down, "Well if that's the case we can all just go over there tomorrow after church and have dinner with her. Baby you can even whip up some of your famous potato salad to take with us." Duran said to Mignon's mom.

"Baby that sounds like a great idea. It's a date. Now let's clean up this mess and go and watch some TV." Mignon knew what that meant. When her mother was high, she needed something to focus on so she would "watch" TV but for the most part, the TV just watched her. Mignon went to her room and called every friend she knew and tried to seek refuge by coming to their house, but they all were either busy or not home. Mignon's heart sank to her stomach but she got an idea in her head that would possibly deter him from raping her. She laid in the bed, pissed her pants and defecated on herself in hopes that he would leave her alone. But when he came to the room that night he was overly brutal because he knew exactly what she was trying to do. He took her curling iron off her dresser, inserted it into her and nearly tore her insides out. When he was through with her, she limped into the bathroom and ran a cold tub of water so that she could soak. Her vagina was throbbing but the cold water soothed her. As she soaked, she thought about killing herself but decided against it because she knew her mother would be devastated. But she did decide that this could no longer go on.

Carolyn Black

I arrived at work Monday morning refreshed. Val laughed heartily at me when she saw me walk through the door. "You thought Zian was a push over huh? Didn't know she was gonna bring it to you like that huh?" She giggled.

"I'm glad you getting a kick out of this." I replied with a smile.

"Yes I am. Now, come meet your new team mate, Candy Fergersen."

"Candy?"

"Yes, Candy. I made some calls and she relocated here from Anisom County DSS. Now you complained about how Zian was so *scary*, well Candy most definitely ain't scary. She's just as fearless as you are."

"Well, whatever. As long as she stays out of my way." I said with a confident laugh. I walked to my desk put my purse down and walked over to where I assumed this *Candy* was. She was standing next to Jenetta engulfed in conversation with her. Oh hell, I thought to myself, this ain't good. When Jenetta saw me coming she gave me a nasty look and rolled her eyes at me. I wanted to slap the taste out of her mouth but with all the trouble I had just gotten into, I kept my cool. I sized Candy up to see if she was going to be a bitch or a team Carolyn player. She was about 5'6, with a coco brown complexion and shoulder length hair that was in a really pretty roller set. She had a nice shape (not nice as mine though) and brown eyes. When she smiled, she had a small gap between her teeth. She was dressed business casual, more so on the plain side. She actually was a pretty woman but I of course was not intimidated at all. I walked right up to her and introduced myself.

"Hello, my name is Carolyn Black. You're Candy right?" I asked as I held my hand out. She greeted me with a smile and very firm handshake. "Damn, this bitch is strong." I thought to myself.

"Yes, I'm Candy. Nice to meet you Carolyn. Jenetta was just telling me about you." I looked at Jenetta with a sarcastic look and replied, "Yea. I bet she was."

My comment appeared to catch Candy off guard but I'm a real bitch and I wasn't going to pretend like I liked Jenetta. So I went ahead and clarified my response to Candy. "Don't worry; me and Jenetta really don't like each other. That's not a secret at all." Now Jenetta's fake ass looked at me as if she was surprised but in my opinion it was because she couldn't believe that I had kept it real instead of being fake like she was trying to be.

"Wow Carolyn." Jenetta laughed uncomfortably. "I didn't know you didn't like me." She said with false modesty.

I simply blew her off and replied, "Whatever Jenetta. You can be fake if you want to but I'm not. Anyway, it's really nice to meet you Candy. If you need anything then my office is right over there." I said as I pointed towards my office.

"Thanks. It's nice to meet you." She said with a look of bewilderment.

"Screw Jenetta", I thought to myself as I walked back over to my desk. "Fake ass, bitch."

Mignon

When Mignon arrived at school Monday morning she was still sore from being raped with her own curling iron. She was at her wits end and made the decision to go straight to the guidance counselor and tell her everything that was going on with her stepfather including the two pregnancies. A rookie fresh out of college, the guidance counselor called Mignon's mother and had her come to the school so that they could discuss what needed to be done. Mignon was petrified but was also relieved that she had told someone besides her diary, all the secrets that she kept down on the inside. When her mother arrived and Mignon told her what was going on, her mother had very little to say to her. She simply told Mignon to get her things because they were going home. Confused, Mignon looked at the guidance counselor who also wore a confused countenance on her face.

Obediently, Mignon gathered her books and headed out the door with her mother. Out in the hallway, where no one was around, Judy slapped Mignon as hard as she could.

"So you're pregnant huh? Well you think your being a little whore with these boys is going to get put on *my husband*? You must have lost your mind. When we get home you are going to pack your shit and get the hell out of my house. You can move in with your grandmother who you *love* and miss so much." Judy said as she mugged the back of Mignon's head as they walked towards the door. Fear gripped Mignon because she knew that Duran was probably going to kill her this time. But she was happy about the possibility of going to live with her grandmother. Anything was better than what she was going through now.

As they were walking out, she felt the need to retrieve her diary from the hiding place she kept it in at school. She lied to her mother and told her that she needed to go to her locker to get her homework. She ran to her hiding spot and retrieved her diary. Once she rejoined her mother, her mother cursed her out the whole way home but she just zoned out; opting to stare out the window. Her mind was running back over all the signs that had been there for her mother to see. But her mother was so far gone on heroin that she couldn't see anything.

When they arrived home, her mother screamed at her to pack her "shit" so she did. Once she'd filled her suitcases to the brim, she sat on her bed waiting for her mother to take her to her grandmother's house. But when her mother came up the steps, she informed Mignon that her grandmother was gone to Raleigh to visit her sister and wouldn't be back until Thursday. Mignon sat on her bed and began sobbing. Her mother stared at her not knowing what to do while trying to read the truth in her daughter's allegations. But her heart, her love and her commitment to her husband wouldn't let her believe her daughter. She'd only seen Duran being good to Mignon. She just couldn't fathom the terrible things that her daughter was telling her. But even if it was true, they could sit down and work this out. She loved her daughter but she loved her husband too. She'd fought for him and he stayed with her even though she couldn't have any more children. Mignon would be eighteen soon and she could be on her own.

She watched her daughter cry and eventually went over to comfort her. Mignon accepted the comfort and hoped that her mother had finally come to her senses. She, however, was sadly mistaken because just as Judy began to caress Mignon's hair, she said, "Baby, I just don't know what to do. I love you but I love your dad to. I can't live without him. We'll all sit down as a family and work this out."

Mignon's heart fell to her stomach and broke into small pieces. She knew that the outcome of a "family meeting" would only be a calamity for her. Her mother only saw the good side of Duran and not that heinous evil side that she knew. Once Judy had left the room, Mignon took out her diary and began to write. She wrote down everything that had happened the past few days including her pregnancy by her stepfather and what had happened today at school. She wrote about her excitement about being able to go live with her grandmother on Thursday and how she would no longer feel like a caged bird. She finished writing and hid her diary in her closet. She laid on the bed, stared at the ceiling and eventually fell asleep from exhaustion. She was awakened by her mother calling her down to dinner. Her deep sleep had almost made her forget the day's events and upcoming "family meeting that was to take place. That was until she got to the bottom of the steps and saw Duran seated in his regular spot reading his paper. He greeted her as usual which meant that her mother hadn't said anything yet. As her mother engaged in her regular routine of setting the table, Mignon looked at her mother with a pleading look in hopes that she would keep what had happened between them. But of course, her mother once again let her down. They discussed it and of course Duran became belligerent and insisted that Mignon was a liar. When he found out that she was pregnant, the color drained from his face. He played it off however as being disappointed in her and angry that she would blame it on him.

After dinner, she was afraid to go to sleep but to her surprise, her mother didn't get high that night which also meant that Duran didn't come to her room. Her fear and expectation that he would eventually come to her room impeded her from going to sleep until almost time to get up for school. She got dressed, grabbed her diary and headed to school. When she got to school she was so tired she could hardly concentrate but she did remember to take her diary out of her book bag and put it in her locker. During lunch, she found a corner and went to sleep. The guidance counselor came got her and took her to her office. Mignon insisted that everything was ok and asked if she could just sleep on her couch for a little while. She blamed her exhaustion on being pregnant and the clueless guidance counselor accepted. Mignon, however, sensing that something may happen to her, made sure that she told her guidance counselor, "If anything ever happens to me, my diary is in my locker, hidden under my gym clothes." The guidance counselor blinked and then looked at Mignon with a suspicious look. Mignon, who was too tired to explain, fell asleep and slept until time to go to basketball practice. She concentrated on playing and wiped her mind clear of everything else.

The next morning, Mignon woke up feeling terrible. She felt so sick that she could barely get out of bed but the rumbling in her stomach sent her to the bathroom to vomit. Hearing her in the bathroom vomiting, Judy came into the bathroom to check on her. Once she saw how pale and ashen Mignon looked, her mother checked her temperature and walked her back to bed. She went downstairs, got a glass of water and some saltine crackers. Being a

PA, she knew that Mignon was probably nauseated due to her pregnancy; therefore she had to be careful about giving her medicine. She sat on the edge of Mignon's bed, gave her the water and fed her the crackers as if Mignon was a toddler. Judy rubbed her hair and comforted her. She insisted that Mignon stay home from school and rest. Judy even volunteered to stay home from work to make sure Mignon was ok. Mignon looked at her mother and for the first time in a long time she felt loved like she'd never felt from her mother. But Mignon insisted that she was ok and could make it to school. She hated being in that house and would much rather be at school sick than at home. After Mignon assured her mother that she was ok, Judy headed on to work. Duran, who had also heard what was going on, drove around the corner as if he was leaving for work. Once he saw Judy pass by, he waited five minutes and drove back to the house. Mignon, who had managed to get in the shower, was in her bedroom drying off when he burst into her room and threw her down on the bed.

"Little bitch! You think you gonna ruin me? Huh? Well, I'll fix you." He spat out as he foamed at the mouth like he was a rabid dog. He ran to her closet, grabbed a wire clothes hanger and pinned Mignon to the bed. He rammed the hanger inside Mignon's vagina and did everything in his power to kill the unborn baby inside of her. *His* unborn baby. Mignon screamed, but the more she struggled, the harder he rammed the hanger inside of her. In a fit of rage, he began choking her until she went unconscious. Scared that he'd killed her, he grabbed a knife and began stabbing her. He then destroyed the house as if a botched robbery had occurred. After the "crime scene" was created to his liking, he cleaned himself up, grabbed all the bloody articles that he'd touched and headed to work. When he arrived, he took the trash bag containing the things from the house and put them in the dumpster behind the office building. He took a deep breath and walked into his job as if nothing had happened.

At Mignon's school, the guidance counselor, who'd been uneasy since Mignon's comment about something happening to her, went to Mignon's first period class to check on her. When she found that Mignon hadn't come to school, she immediately went to talk with the assistant principal. The assistant principal, who was livid, immediately called Fosterberg CPS and made a report.

Carolyn Black

"Fosterberg County Department of Social Services, this is Carolyn Black."

"Ms. Black this is Julia Mabin, assistant principal at East Haven High School and I've got a situation that I feel demands an urgent response." She filled me in on a story about a student who'd reported that her stepfather was molesting her and had gotten her pregnant. She was concerned because the student hadn't come to school today. She also informed me that the child had made the report several days ago to the guidance counselor who had not taken the necessary steps. Although she told me that the guidance counselor was new and fresh out of college, I was still very pissed because mandatory reporting was social work 101. Hell, it was common sense 101.

Because of the dire circumstances I didn't want to waste time letting her have it for waiting so long to make a report. So I got the address, grabbed Candy and headed to the child's home. I briefed Candy on the ride over there as I hauled ass to get there. I had a bad feeling about this one and wanted to get there as soon as possible.

When we arrived, I got a really eerie feeling because the front door was slightly ajar. Candy, who was a dare devil went straight to the door and was getting ready to walk in.

"Candy, don't go in there! This shit doesn't look right." I exclaimed.

"Girl forget that, something fishy is going on and we can't wait for the police to get here."

"Fosterberg DSS. Is anyone here?" She called out as she cautiously pushed the door open. I didn't want to show it, but I was scared. I usually was the hard one but I also wasn't crazy and didn't know if some psycho was still in the house. Nevertheless I reluctantly followed her in. The house was trashed and so I immediately got on my phone and called 911. I didn't feel comfortable being in there so I tried to grab Candy's hand and pull her out of the house. But as I turned to walk out the door, I heard a faint moan coming from upstairs. Candy who'd also heard the moan ran upstairs so I followed her. What we found sent shock waves through my body causing my legs and hands to shake uncontrollably. Lying on the bed was a mangled teenage girl who was covered in a pool of blood, barely hanging on to her life. I called 911 again and told them that we needed an ambulance immediately.

"Baby, hang in there. Help is on the way. My name is Candy and I'm a social worker. Who did this to you?" She said as she held the young girl's hand. The girl, whose name was Mignon, tried to speak but when she opened her mouth, nothing came out but a spurt of blood. When the police and ambulance arrived they rolled Mignon out on the stretcher and headed to the hospital. Candy and I followed them to the hospital. We were both silent, taking in what we'd just seen. We both felt terrible because in our minds we were both thinking the same thing, the stepfather was responsible for this. Neither of us could prove it but we felt that it was too much of a coincidence that Mignon was brutally attached within days of revealing the pregnancy and abuse. I looked over at Candy; who was quickly wiping away tears before they threatened to slide down her cheek and grabbed her hand to let her know that I empathized with her. When we arrived at the hospital, a police officer was there waiting to question us all while Mignon was in surgery. We filled him in on what the assistant principal had told me over the phone. The officer immediately alerted the doctors to check for signs of pregnancy and sent someone to find the stepfather. Mignon's mother, whose name was Judy, arrived shortly after we did. She came in towards the conclusion of our conversation as Candy and I filled the police in on what we'd seen and heard from the school. Initially she was distraught and demanded to see her daughter and find out what had happened to her. But at the mention of her husband's name in relation to possibly being the culprit, she immediately became livid.

"I'm sorry... are you all trying to accuse my husband of doing this to my daughter? He would never harm her. That stupid guidance counselor had no business contacting you. I love my daughter dearly but she's mixed up. I think she got pregnant by some knuckle head boy at school and instead of owning up to it, she blamed my husband. I asked him about it and he said he didn't have anything to do with it and *I* believe him!" She snapped and then turned to go into the operating room where they were working on Mignon. I felt my face turning red. The nerve of this bitch. But before I could respond, Candy; who apparently was just as much of a fire cracker as I was, was already preparing to let the woman have it. I grabbed her hand and gave her the, "calm down, we are professionals" look. I couldn't believe it because *I* was usually the one who had to be calmed down. Candy adhered to my look and retreated back to her seat because technically our job was done here. Since the child was in the hospital as a result of being attacked, we were out of our jurisdiction until the police did their investigation and located the perpetrator. Once they determined that, then it would be our job to have the child placed in a safe environment.

"Carolyn, I need to step out and get some fresh air before I go postal up in this bitch. I can't believe that this bitch is more focused on that piece of shit man than her own daughter who is in there fighting for her life." Candy whispered so that no one would hear her.

"Come on, let's go grab some lunch." I said as I gently grabbed her arm and led her outside. As we were leaving out two women stopped us at the emergency room entrance. Assuming that they saw our badges and realized that we were DSS, they wanted to talk to us.

"Ms. Black?" A tall blonde woman who appeared to be in her forties, with green eyes and a thin frame that was clothed in an olive green suit asked.

"Yes, I'm Carolyn Black." I replied as she held her hand out for me to shake.

"Hello. I'm Julia Mabin, assistant principal at East Haven High School and this is Laura Hines, the guidance counselor." She said with a look of disgust as she introduced Laura. Laura being fully aware of the cause of the disgust dropped her head. She appeared to be very young, maybe twenty two years old. She also had blonde hair but she had sky blue eyes and was about a foot shorter. She was also dressed professionally over her thin frame.

"Nice to meet you, this is my partner, Candy Fergersen." I replied.

"Well I hate to be having to meet you under these circumstances." Julia said, holding on to her look of disgust. "How is she doing?"

We really don't know what her current condition is because she's still in surgery." I answered. Laura shifted from side to side as tears began to slide down her cheeks.

Speaking for the first time since the introductions she said, "Words can't express how terrible and ignorant I feel. This is all my fault. If I had acted sooner this wouldn't have happened."

Speaking out of anger, frustration and disgust, Julia, the principal responded, "Yes Laura, there is the possibility that this could have been prevented if you had reported this sooner." She pointed her finger and began to wag it. "But it's not your fault because we all know that it was that sonofabitch stepfather of hers who did this. But let this be a harsh lesson for you. When a child tells you something that extreme, you must contact DSS. This is your first year and you thought you were doing the right thing by calling her mom. But for future references, always call DSS to report any abuse or neglect and then contact the parents next."

"I understand. I just thought that her mother would handle it. She seemed so sincere and focused on her daughter." She responded while still holding her head down. I felt so sorry for her because I knew that she was carrying a great weight on her shoulders. Although she could have done things differently, playing the blame game wasn't going to change anything so I offered for them to go with us to lunch in order to begin piecing the story together. They agreed and we headed to a small café a few blocks away from the hospital.

After telling me and Candy word for word what Mignon had said, the counselor seemed to have an epiphany. "Oh my God, I just remembered that she said that she kept a diary and that if anything happened to her then her diary was in her locker at school." Grateful for the information, we made sure to report it to the police officer when we arrived back at the hospital. We looked around for Mignon's mother but could not find her. When we asked where she was, we were informed that she had gone down to the police station where they were holding her husband for questioning. At that point I think we all had to same look on our faces, disgust and disbelief. We all agreed that if this child pulled through this, we would make sure that she never had to be around those people that she called parents again.

We all sat down and waited for a report. Candy paced back and forth, Laura sat anxiously bouncing her leg up and down, Julia sat staring off into space and I sat back and just observed everything and everybody. While waiting, we did receive news that the police had found the diary in Mignon's locker at school. We all felt a sense of relief, until the doctor came in and told us that they'd lost Mignon on the operating table. We all sat there in a daze for what seemed like forever. Laura broke the silence when she let out a loud tear filled scream. Instead of looking at her like she was crazy, we all joined her in some kind of way whether it was loud sobs or silent tears. I personally chose the silent tears because I wasn't big on showing my emotions in front of people.

"Well, I bet this wasn't what you expected to have to deal with on your second day here huh? Welcome to Fosterberg County." I said sullenly as Candy and I rode back to the office to gather our things and complete our paperwork.

"I have dealt with some terrible things but this by far has been the worse. I'm going to need a drink." She said in a half-heartedly manner. I shook my head and replied, "Well honey join the club because most of us are already alcoholics because of this job. I will gladly gather the crew together and head to the bar when we get done."

"And I will gladly accept." She replied dryly.

I honestly wanted more than a drink and preferred to be in the comfort of my own home so that I could meet up with my best friend Mary Jane whom I loved dearly. Hell, I had a bottle of wine at home that I could drink on all night without worrying about having to drive home. But I knew that all this was new for Candy and I wanted to be there to make her feel more comfortable. It was a terrible thing that she had walked into on her second day and I knew that my co-workers and I always leaned on one another when we were dealing with these types of situations. So I gathered the crew together; even Jenetta's hatin' ass and headed to our favorite down time spot Jar Bar. While we were there, I got a call from Brad asking me to accompany him on a two day vacation to New York for the upcoming weekend. Of course I jumped at the idea because I needed a vacation and I needed a good screw as well because I didn't have Jermaine I mean Avery anymore. Demarcus was who knows where and Dewayne's itty, bitty, teeny, weeney wasn't what I needed at that point and time. I needed a long hard banging that would knock me out of reality for a while and I knew that Brad could hold his own in that area plus who knew what kinds of gifts he would lavish me with once we arrived in New York.

After a few drinks and some food, we all called it a night. I went home to Mary Jane and a hot tub of water. I packed a bag for my trip to NY and as I was packing, to my surprise I also got a phone call from Demarcus. He told me that his wife and son had gone to visit family in Elizabeth City which freed him up to come and see me that night. I was still pissed at him so I tried to play hard to get. I wanted him to beg, which he did. I eventually "gave in" and told him he could come by. I was excited because he always knew what to say to make me laugh and feel better. Plus his sexual healing was highly welcomed so I hurriedly bathed myself in anticipation of his arrival. I knew that when he left I would have to soak in vinegar to tighten up my Juicy before I met with Brad because what I planned to lay on Demarcus after the day I'd had was definitely going to require some nipping and tucking...and most definitely some soaking.

Case #32486 The Mind of the Molester

BaLing wiped the steam off the bathroom mirror and stared intently at herself as pain and anguish slowly crept over her body and began to permeate beyond her flesh into the inner most part of her bones. She felt pain unlike any other pain that she'd ever been subjected to in her life. Sadness, hurt and betrayal were not unfamiliar to her but the current manner in which she was experiencing those things was so extreme that words could not describe them. The mental angst made her ache physically. Her chest felt heavy, her head ached, she had trouble catching her breath and her heart felt like it was literally breaking. She felt loneliness; she felt extreme fear and an over powering sense of rage; which was an emotion that was new to her because she'd suppressed it for most of her life. The difference was; in the past she'd never known true love and now that she'd had it and lost it she could no longer hold in *any* of the emotions that had currently overtaken her body. The only person who had ever loved her; her husband Henry, was dead and now she was getting ready to have his baby. Her water had already broke but she just couldn't make herself turn away from the mirror to go and call for help. She just kept looking at herself so that she could figure out what it was that she'd done to deserve the cards of life that she'd been dealt. It was as if God was playing a dirty trick on her whereby He'd pacify her with intervals of happiness and just as she would start to relax, He would pull the rug from under her with soul crushing experiences that would forever be etched into her brain. She let out a blood curdling scream and slammed her fist through the cheap mirror; shattering it. She slid down the bathroom wall, sobbing uncontrollably; negating the blood that was seeping down her arm. She curled up into a fetal position and laid there thinking about her life: all the hurt, all the pain and all the disappointments. She looked up towards the ceiling and questioned God as to why she'd even been born. Why had He put her here to endure all this pain? She had only met God through Henry and had grown to love Him. Now she was starting to hate Him and wish that she'd never met Him at all.

She closed her eyes as her 23 years of life flooded back into her memory. Her Korean mother had been forced to give BaLing away when she was three months old because her grandparents threatened to disown her mother if she kept BaLing. Her father; who was black, never knew that she existed because her grandparents wouldn't let her mother have anything to do with him once they'd found out about their relationship. So after BaLing was born; they'd insisted that BaLing be given up for adoption to an affluent white family who was looking for a child because they couldn't have children of their own.

Her childhood started out being everything that a typical child could want. Her parents doted over her and gave her the world. They bought her things, took her places and gave her everything she wanted. They never hid the fact that she was adopted from her but she didn't start to realize what being adopted meant until she noticed how other parents treated their kids. They were affectionate and loving, warm and attentive. Her parents; on the other hand, were a young couple in their early twenties who were like hippies so they were liberal and more like her friends than parents. She was allowed to run freely around the house with her crayons or markers in her hands; coloring throughout the duration of her run. She could speak her mind, pick out her own clothes, wear her hair wild and pretty much do anything she wanted as long as she didn't endanger herself. They taught her to be liberated and even started teaching her about her body; all the while negating to teach her discipline and give her genuine, unconditional love. It was as if there was a transparent barrier; a palpable boundary between them that allowed them to be good to her, show her compassion and keep her happily entertained but kept them from actually *loving* her. There was warmth and sporadic moments of intimacy but there were very few hugs and kisses.

By the time she was six she was fully aware of the lack of parental attachment between her and her parents but she accepted it because she knew she was adopted and *that* permitted her parents to treat her differently. And since they had no information on how to locate her biological family she took comfort in knowing that she had a home and decent people that would at least take care of her. But the crushing blow came with the realization that not only was she adopted but she also *looked* differently than everyone else within her surroundings. She remembered being on the playground when one of the kids asked her "if she tasted like chocolate" because her skin "looked like someone had covered her with chocolate milk." It was at that point that she began to recognize the drastic difference in her skin tone in comparison to her parents' and the people they interacted with. It was also at that point whereby she'd started recognizing how differently the other people treated her. The kids she played with in the neighborhood only played with her because their parents made them and they felt sorry for the "poor little brown girl." People were always overly nice to her, trying to make sure she felt comfortable, even catering to her. And her parents did a great job of showing her off and parading her around; treating her more like a pet than their child. People pitied their inability to have kids but patted them on the back and glorified them for adopting "a nonwhite" baby. They were always so impressed by their generosity because BaLing was "such an unfortunate creature who was destined to have a life of strife and adversity had they not rescued her."

Although her parents had always taught her to be original, liberated and in touch with her inner self; they never prepared her to be comfortable with her "outer self". They never really discussed race as it pertained to her thus leaving her extremely unprepared for the upward battle that she was going to be facing once she entered middle school. She'd gotten through elementary school because she was cute and feisty. People felt sorry for her, embraced her with false modesty and made her their personal charity case thus causing her to have a false sense of security. They applauded everything she did; ooed and awed over even her smallest accomplishments and frequently let her bend the rules, "because she had special needs." But once elementary school was over life became very difficult for her because her peers were no longer forced to include her anymore and no one was willing to accommodate her based off her cuteness and hard knock life. She didn't know anything about being Black or Asian and the White kids most definitely didn't look at her as one of them, therefore she found herself feeling insecure and totally isolated. She didn't know who she was or where she fit in. The kids were cruel, the teachers were inattentive and she sustained some type of bullying or taunting on a daily basis. Being strong willed and "free spirited" she initially tried to stand up for herself and fight back. However, the kids only used that against her, making her appear to be loud and aggressive; almost comical and entertaining. She had no friends with the exception of an Asian girl who eventually moved away just as BaLing had started to form a solid bond with her. She rarely attended parties or sleepovers and when she did, they made her the brunt of their jokes and played cruel tricks on her. So with each passing grade, her free spirit began to diminish and her outspokenness became muted. She eventually gave in and tried everything in her power to assimilate herself thus abandoning her originality by trying to look like them, act like them and blend in with them but nothing worked.

At home, BaLing's relationship with her parents was also changing based off her transition into adolescence. While they didn't protect her from the abuse that she sustained from her peers and their parents; they did begin paying more attention to her; making it a point to tell her on a daily basis how beautiful she was becoming. They urged her to find "spiritual healing" within her body by joining them in their daily, "meditation sessions" whereby they would lay naked in the outdoors and touch themselves. Because BaLing had witnessed her parents' "daily ritual" throughout her childhood, she felt that it was normal and since they had secluded her from themselves intimately for so long she was obliged to join them. She felt like they were finally letting her into their bubble; thus giving her the special attention that she needed. They started letting her sleep in the bed with them as if she were a toddler but the difference was that they would all engage in their "meditation sessions" and cuddle while sleeping naked. The sporadic moments of warmth also increased to frequent gestures of intimacy. The hugs were tighter and the kisses longer; to the point whereby she felt that they were finally growing to love her and see her as their daughter. She began to cling to them and hang on their every word; forming an unhealthy dependence on them. And it appeared that the more dependent on them she became the more loving and attentive they were to her. Little did she know they there were fattening her up for the kill.

A contraction hit BaLing's stomach so hard that she sat straight up and was jolted back into the present. She knew that she had to get to the hospital but she was too weak to get up and make her way to the phone. But she did however rip off a piece of her shirt so that she could wrap her hand up. Once her hand was secure, she laid her head back against the wall and let her memories take over her again. By the time she was twelve she started realizing that although her parents acted as though they were hippies, they; in actuality, were imposters trying mask their deviant desires to do drugs, have sex freely and "stand for a cause." They were nothing more than wanna bees. Both had grown up as white trash but once her adopted mother had gotten rich off of her grandparent's inheritance the two had gotten married and vowed to live by the laws of: carpe diem, nirvana and anarchy. They'd moved into a lavish neighborhood by which *they* didn't belong and tried to fit in with the other wealthy people. They found that although their financial status wasn't going to get them into any social circles; drugs and free love would so they assumed the role as hippies and lived in marital bliss until they tried to have a child. And although they tried everything from fertility drugs to putting "sacred rocks" under their bed; BaLing's adopted mother couldn't get pregnant. And when she found out that BaLing's grandmother was looking for a home for BaLing, she jumped at the idea. The adoption was just what they needed to catapult them into their desired social status and give them an induction into the oldest, most prominent and most established social club; that being "club parenthood." They got to rub elbows with soccer moms and golfing dads, teachers, lawyers, doctors and the most elite of the elite thus giving them access and exposure to tea parties and poker games and all other social groups and clubs. In the mist of some of their "elbow rubbing", her parents found that there were many parents who used drugs and liked the "swinger" lifestyle; therefore; they formed a secret society and started having parties weekly whereby the drugs flowed freely and the sex was random. They called the gatherings "free lay" parties by which the attendees did ecstasy, smoked pot, snorted cocaine and had orgies. The attendees all had sex in one room and when they were done having sex with one person, they were "free to lay" with anyone else and could do a "partner swap". By the time BaLing turned twelve; she was smoking pot and drinking liquor. And since she was very in tune with her body and had known how to "please herself" by the time she was ten, joining in on the "free to lay" portion of the parties was inevitable. Her first experience came when she was thirteen. She wasn't afraid because her parents had been prepping her; unbeknownst to her, for the majority of her short lived life. She was very comfortable with her body and since her and her parents touched each other frequently, being touched by others didn't faze her. They only had to do a little coaxing and since they were finally starting to be so attentive and affectionate, she willingly obliged to anything that was put before her by her parents. They started her out slow and would only allow oral sex to be performed on her and vice versa. But by the time she was fifteen all that began to change. She was highly desired by all because of her youthfulness and exotic beauty. She had sex with older men, younger men and their wives or girlfriends therefore she learned a lot about sex and pleasing others. She became so highly demanded that people would wait in line to have sex with her. Being at the "free lay" parties boosted her self esteem and made her feel like she was on top of the world. She was good at what she did and people respected her. They desired her, worshipped her and treated her like she was a star.

There were times during "partner swaps" by which she ended up having sex with her adopted parents but her relationship became so ambivalent with them outside of the "free lay" parties that she didn't know whether she was coming or going. They were parents when it came to things like homework and chores but by the end of the night, they were all high and making love. And the more and more her shattered ego and self esteem were fueled by the power she possessed within her "free lay" lifestyle the less and less she started caring about school and life outside of her home. And since she viewed herself as being nothing more than a big black stain that oozed throughout her school and community, she really didn't think anyone would notice. People; however did start to notice and her parents; being the social butterflies that they were, would die before they allowed her to embarrass them or compromise their budding positions in the elite social circles therefore they made it point to push her to do better in school. They depended on her to maintain their social status and they knew she depended on them for survival thus igniting an ominous dance of codependency. A dance that eventually became unbalanced when jealousy began to overcome BaLing's adoptive mother due to all of the attention that BaLing was getting from the partiers as well as BaLing's adoptive father. She began mistreating BaLing by turning her into her personal slave and if BaLing didn't do what she was supposed to do, her mother would beat her mercilessly.
The thought of the lash of the whip her mother used to beat her with coincided with another contraction and she knew that the baby was coming whether she wanted it to or not. She cried out in pain and began crawling into the bedroom to get the phone. As she crawled to the bed her mind flashed back to the many times that her mother would make her get down on her hands and knees and eat her food from a bowl on the floor as if she were an animal. But the pivotal point of her life came when her mother took a whip and beat BaLing across her back during one of the free to lay parties. BaLing knew that although her mother had tried to make it appear

to be a kinky sexual escapade but in actuality she wanted to punish BaLing and took great pleasure in beating her. However, her mother had gone too far and when BaLing had gone to school the next day her teacher noticed the blood on the back of her shirt and sent her to the school nurse. When the nurse saw the lash marks on BaLing's back, she'd called DSS.

BaLing remembered that a very nice social worker named Carolyn Black had come to the hospital and interviewed her. BaLing, who at that point in her fifteen year old life was tired of the lying and confusion, had finally let everything off her chest. The social worker, who was very pretty and fair skinned, turned bright red as BaLing had told her about the sex and beatings going on in her home. After that, her parents had been arrested and BaLing had been put into foster care. She remembered that the Social Worker had attempted to locate her biological parents but had been unable to do so. And although BaLing had been removed from the codependent grasp of her parents, the damage had been done and the yearnings never left her body. All she knew to do was to use sex as a means of empowerment therefore most of her placements were terminated prematurely because she would end up having sex with her male foster parents or her foster brothers. She was known as the school slut at her high schools because she would sleep with any and everybody to get what she needed or wanted. She had even slept with girls if there was some sort of mental, physical gain or monetary.

As BaLing held onto her stomach and fought through another painful contraction, she thought about her old social worker Carolyn Black. Carolyn had been very special to her because although she was tough on BaLing, she'd never judged her. She'd always told BaLing that her behavior was a response to the things her parents had done to her. However, she also told BaLing that she was now old enough to begin taking responsibility and be held accountable for her actions. Carolyn referred her to a therapist who was a fifty year old Black woman who didn't take any shit. She; Dr. Weaver, was also very tough on BaLing but she was very understanding and BaLing trusted her. Dr. Weaver taught her how to understand healthy relationships and boundaries and how not to see love as being equivalent to sex. After she'd been seeing Dr. Weaver for a few months and had begun attending a different high school, BaLing started making progress. Dr. Weaver helped her to see her worth and to be able to look beyond what she could do in the bedroom. BaLing had begun to realize that she was very smart in school, had a knack for playing the piano and was able to make friends with girls and boys in a healthy manner. She'd even been able to get an after school job working at McDonalds.

Not being able to stand another contraction, BaLing dialed 911 and waited for the ambulance to arrive. She began crying because she knew that she was getting ready to bring this baby into the world without her precious Henry. As she laid there waiting for the ambulance to come, she smiled as she thought about Henry, the love of her life, the only man who hadn't tried to take advantage of her. They had met at the high school she was attending not long after she'd turned seventeen. She had been new at the school and was determined to make a fresh start; therefore she did everything in her power to avoid boys. About three months into the semester, she'd been coming out of class and while looking down at her watch, she ran head first right into Henry. They'd hit it off and had began dating. BaLing was so afraid of being in a relationship with Henry because she'd never been in a healthy relationship with a male before and she was afraid that her sexual deviance would ruin things between them. She told all these things to Dr. Weaver who took this as an opportunity to teach her the appropriate way to handle a platonic relationship. Unbeknownst to Henry, Dr. Weaver had walked BaLing through the entire development of their relationship because BaLing told Dr. Weaver everything about their relationship all the way down to their first kiss.

After about three or four months of dating, Dr. Weaver gave BaLing her stamp of approval for Henry because, Henry had been great to her, and because he was a devout Christian, he did not believe in premarital sex. Henry took BaLing to church with him and taught her about God. His family loved her and embraced her. BaLing was afraid of Henry finding out about her past but one day after church as she waited for the group home van to come pick her up, she'd told him that she needed to talk to him. She'd talked to Dr. Weaver first before telling Henry anything. Dr. Weaver had responded by telling BaLing that she was proud of her but this was a decision that she would have to make on her own. Dr. Weaver however had made it a point to warn BaLing of the potential consequences that could come from her telling Henry about her past and she'd also encouraged BaLing to be prepared for the possibility of a breakup. BaLing considered all these things but she felt that she owed it to Henry to tell him the truth. So one day, with Dr. Weaver's encouragement, the group home had allowed Henry to come over for a day visit. Sitting in the back yard at the picnic table, BaLing had spilled her guts about everything that had happened to her in her life. She'd spared Henry from the gory details but was very blunt about having sex with her parents as well as numerous boys *and girls* in her past. She'd told him about seeing Dr. Weaver and how he was the first stable, healthy relationship that she'd ever had with a man. After telling him these things, he'd sat there quietly without speaking. She'd began crying as she waited for him to either break up with her or force her to show him some of the kinky tricks she'd learned. She'd worried that he would look at her like a whore but contrary to her beliefs, he'd stood up, walked around to her side of the table and hugged her. He'd told her that he loved her regardless of her past and that God loved her no matter what she'd done. He then wiped her tears away, grabbed her hands and began praying over her. She'd never felt the love that she'd felt at that point and time in her life. No orgasm had ever made her feel as good as she'd felt then.

As they'd prepared to graduate, Henry prepared to go to Winston-Salem State University and he encouraged BaLing to follow. BaLing didn't think twice about obliging Henry once Carolyn; her social worker, had made it possible for her to get a scholarship and grant money so that she didn't have to worry about paying for school. Once they'd begun attending school together, the two were inseparable and decided to get married their senior year.

Despite the intensity of her contractions, BaLing managed to giggle as she thought about how Henry had asked her to marry him. They'd been walking from class after one of the biggest snow storms they'd ever witnessed. They were walking up a hill and had started having a snow ball fight. In the midst of the fight, he'd tripped and went rolling down the hill. When he hit the bottom of the hill, he looked like the abominable snow man. She'd laughed so hard that she'd almost pissed her pants until she noticed him frantically digging through the snow as if he'd lost something. Finally he found what he was looking for and she saw that it was a little black box. With his plans of a romantic proposal ruined, he decided to go ahead and propose to her right then and there. She'd laughed but gladly accepted.

They were married a few months later and moved into a small apartment off campus. She remembered that she had been so afraid of having sex with him on their wedding night. But very much to her delight, he'd made love to her like she'd never been made love to before. He was very sensual and gentle with her. The orgasm that she'd experienced that night was unlike any other because it was an orgasm that not only came from sexual penetration but from love as well. For the first few months of their marriage, she'd held back her "freaky" desires due to her fear that he would look at her like a slut. But Henry; who was no longer obligated by his faith to withstand any sexual activities, was just as sexual as she was. And being that he was new to "sex" he encouraged her to do whatever she felt was comfortable. From that point on, she and Henry began having some of the best sex she'd ever had in her life. He was so in love with her and he had such a high desire for her that they had sex almost every day; sometimes more than once a day. Both of their sexual appetites for each other were insatiable. And for once in her life she'd felt good about her sexual appetite because it was finally with the right person. Initially they were dirt poor but nevertheless they were the happiest people in the world. They'd decided to put off having a baby until they both had been working their jobs for at least a year. Eventually he'd gotten a job as a school teacher and she was starting her career as a nurse. And just as they'd planned, after they'd both been on their jobs for a year, she'd gotten pregnant. They both were ecstatic and couldn't wait for the arrival of their baby boy, Henry Jr. They'd been very proactive in planning and arranging for the baby's future. They purchased life insurance, started a college fund and made sure to get a high quality health insurance plan. What they didn't plan for was the drunk driver that hit Henry while he was on his way home from a parent teacher meeting at his school. At the time of the accident, BaLing had been seven months pregnant and when she'd found out about Henry's death, she'd also wanted to die. A part of her did die, but the only thing that kept her going was the anticipation of the arrival of Henry Jr.

As the memories continued to flood her mind, she began to sob. She thought about how God had robbed her of her happiness. She wanted to scream and curse Him, but the intense pain she was feeling wouldn't allow her to. She tried to pull herself together as she heard the faint sound of sirens coming from outside. She forced herself up off the bed, grabbed her and Henry's wedding picture and picked up her overnight bag. She waddled slowly to the front door and almost fell over as another contraction ricocheted throughout her stomach and back. She heard a loud bang on the door and gladly welcomed the first responders.

They helped her into the ambulance and transported her to the hospital. Henry Jr. was born at 5 a.m. and weighed 7lbs 5 oz. She cried when she looked down into that precious little face. Henry Jr. looked so much like his father that it almost scared her. Henry's parents were there when she gave birth and were very proud grandparents. They all shared a moment of tears as they all thought about what they had lost as well as what they had gained. After they'd left for the day, the nurse came in to talk to BaLing about breast feeding. Although BaLing was a nurse herself, she still felt very ignorant and inferior when it came to having a newborn baby. The nurse showed her how to get the baby to latch on and how to hold his head so that he could properly get the milk. Once the nurse was confident that she'd shown BaLing what to do she left the mother to spend some alone time with her child, promising to come back in to check on her. BaLing did well with the baby and was a doting mother. Henry's parents returned later on in the evening and spent more time with her. By the end of the night, she was tired and near delirious. But her motherly duties took precedence over her fatigue, therefore when Henry Jr. began to cry she pulled out her breast and began breastfeeding him. As she looked at her baby, she saw Henry Sr. and for a brief moment; in the midst of her delirium, she thought that it was Henry Sr. sucking on her breast as he'd done many times before. She closed her eyes and then not only was she envisioning Henry Sr., she also saw the faces of her adoptive father and mother as well as the faces of all the other people she'd slept with. Her body began to get hot and as her baby sucked on her breast she began to get extremely aroused. In her mind he began sucking harder and the harder he sucked the more aroused she became. She took her hand and began to massage her vagina. Soon, before she knew it, she was having an orgasm. After her baby stopped sucking, she looked down at him and felt ashamed of herself. But she blamed it on her delirium and bereavement. Finally they both drifted off to sleep.

Later on in the night, the nurse returned to check on her and Henry Jr. And once the nurse who'd came in to check on them left, Henry Jr. began to cry again. She knew it was time to feed him again but she became overwhelmed with fear because she didn't want what happened earlier to happen again. She took a deep breath and laughed at herself. "BaLing, you're tripping." She said aloud as she pulled her breast out to feed the baby. However, as soon as she put her breast back into the baby's mouth the same feelings came back. And the harder she tried to fight them, the more relentless they became. She saw the same faces in her mind and began getting aroused again. She couldn't resist putting her hand back inside her vagina. Her body became so hot for penetration that she began looking around the room for something she could stick inside of herself. She settled on the thin nursing baby bottle that the hospital had given her to put milk into.

As the baby sucked on her breast, she took the nipple off the bottle and stuck the bottle inside her vagina. She thrust the bottle in and out until orgasm overtook her body. At that point she went out of her mind. She looked down at the innocent baby sucking on her breast and saw his father. She took her breast out of his mouth and began kissing his little body in a way that a mother should never kiss a baby. She worked her way down to his little penis and lifted it up to put it into her mouth. As she opened her mouth to make contact with his penis, the baby began peeing in her face, which snapped her back into reality. Thinking to herself, "touché little man, touché" she continued to allow him to pee in her face until he was finished as punishment for what she'd done to him. She got up, washed her face and washed Henry Jr. up as well. She rocked him to sleep and went to her overnight bag. She pulled out the picture of her and Henry and sobbed uncontrollably.

"Henry, you've gotta help me. I'm scared Henry. I can't live without you. You are the only person that could help me. You're the only person that's ever loved me and now you're gone, I can't handle it Henry. Oh my God. I almost molested my own son Henry and I know it was you and God that stopped me. I can't ruin his life like my mine was ruined." She cried. And then; as if being hit by a ton of bricks, she knew what she had to do. She went over to her sleeping baby, made sure that he was safe in his basinet and bent down and kissed him like a mother was supposed to kiss her baby. She packed her things up; left a note instructing the nurse to make sure that Henry Jr. went with his grandparents and snuck out of the hospital.

Candy

When Carolyn walked through the door, the smell of her sweet perfume hit my nose. I froze as I turned to look at her. She looked flawless, wearing a black blazer that hit the top of her wide but perfectly proportioned hips. She wore a leopard print blouse under the jacket, fitted black slacks and black peep toe pumps. Her hair was wild and curly and her pouty, full lips sported bright red lipstick. As she strolled through the room with that fierce poise and confident walk, it seemed as if everything else around her stopped. No one moved because we all were in such awe of her. We were mere mortals and she was the goddess of all things beautiful and powerful. Envy crept from the bottom of my feet to the ends of my hair follicles until I had succumbed to it. Although I have no doubts or insecurities about myself she made me feel ugly and inferior. I hated her. But at the same time I had a passion and desire for her that I couldn't explain. I was in a constant state of ambivalence: envy, admiration; competition, submission; loathing and unfathomable attraction. I didn't know whether to have an orgasm or hit her. I'm not a lesbian but the feelings I have for Carolyn are unnatural. I mean, at first it was all about the competition and showing her and everyone else that I was a just as good if not a better social worker than she was. But in my pursuit of out doing her, I've become captivated by her. I'm enchanted by her and I want her to notice me in ways that she has never noticed me before. I want her respect and I desire her approval. But when I'm around her I keep my poker face on at all times because she's like the popular girl at school and I'm the new kid who just wants to be in her presence. I am a woman with pride and I will bow down to no one but it's something about this woman that has altered my way of thinking and being. My secret hatred for her has turned into desire and my desire has turned into...lust. I want to see her naked. I want to roll around in bed with her, I want to taste her juices and make her scream. I want to turn her out and bite her until it hurts. I despise her for making me feel this way but I despise myself more for not being able to resist whatever spell it is that she has on me and everyone else.

Carolyn Black

"Fosterberg County Department of Social Services, Carolyn Black speaking."

"Hi Ms. Black. This is Jonetta Green with the Fosterberg County Hospital. We have a baby here that has been left in the hospital." I gasped as I thought about a precious little baby being left alone at the hospital. But then again, I had to rethink that. At least the baby was in one of the safest possible places and from what I'd seen in my days as a social worker, maybe this was one of the best possible things that this mother could have done for her child. So many parents took their kids home and abused them or neglected them, in some cases even *killed* them. Maybe this mom actually realized before it was too late that she wasn't capable of being a good parent.

"I'm on my way." I responded. I went and grabbed Candy and we both rode over to the hospital. After collecting information about the mother and the baby, I learned that the mother was a child that used to be on my caseload a long time ago. BaLing Haun's story was one that I would never forget. I shuddered at what that child had been through and even more when I learned about the recent death of her husband. I knew that BaLing had been severely sexually abused and as a result had been extremely sexually reactive. Who knows why that girl left that baby at the hospital, but I had a feeling that it was probably for the best.

No one knew where BaLing was, but the note that she had left instructed us to have the baby placed with the grandparents who were all too willing to take the baby. After conducting a background check and home visit, our team along with the grandparents had a Child and Family meeting. We all came to the decision that the grandparents would keep the baby until we found out exactly what was going on with BaLing. We tried contacting her at her house but of course she wasn't there. I had no idea how to find her and figured for the most part that she probably didn't want to be found anyway. Of course we contacted the police and put out a missing person's report and I really hoped that we would find her because I had a connection to BaLing. I had started working with her when I was a fresh new social worker and wet behind the ears. I had done everything in my power to help her and once I found out that she had gone off to college and gotten married, I figured that she was ok but apparently I was wrong.

Candy

I had to figure out a way to lure Carolyn into my lair. I

couldn't take it any longer so I began to concoct a plot to get her to my house so I could seduce her. I decided to have a party at my house and invite the crew from work. I would have food, drinks and good music. I planned to get Carolyn drunk and then slip her a roofie. Then once she was passed out I would have my way with her. I knew I was becoming borderline psycho but it was like I had no control of my own mind or body. My insatiable passion for Carolyn was the only driving force that was guiding my rationality. So I began working on my scheme and spread the word to our small group friends. I didn't want too many people there because that would be more people for me to have to get rid of. I only invited Mario, Val and her husband, Jenetta, Carolyn and a few other people from work. I scheduled the party for the upcoming Saturday, around 8:30 p.m.

On the day of the party, I worked feverishly to make sure that everything was perfect. I knew Carolyn liked potato skins smothered in cheese and bacon so I made sure that they were on the menu. I also prepared hot wings, a seven layer dip, meatballs and a veggie tray. I made a fruit tray with fresh blue berries, honey dew melon, pineapples and strawberries. As I whipped up the fruit dip that would accommodate the fruit tray, I began to get turned on thinking about how I wanted to spread it all over Carolyn's breast and slowly lick every morsel of it off her. I closed my eyes and squeezed my vagina muscles together as an orgasm began trying to sneak its way out of my walls. "Get it together Candy." I thought to myself. "Am I crazy?" I said aloud to myself. "What the hell is wrong with me? I'm not gay. What has this woman done to me?" I moaned as I grabbed the edge of the counter while shaking my head. I took a deep breath and thought to myself, "I really have lost it. I don't do all this shit for a man so why in the world am I going to all this trouble for a woman who I know is not going to reciprocate my feelings?"

With that thought, I started to become apprehensive. "Fuck this. I'm just going to call the whole thing off." I mumbled as I stirred the punch, while trying to talk some sense into myself. By the time the punch was finished, I'd about talked myself out of it;

that is until my door bell rang and I saw Carolyn standing there. All my rationality and thoughts of me being psycho dissipated, never to return again. I checked my watch and realized that it was 8:00.

"Damnit!" I thought to myself. I wasn't even dressed and here Carolyn was standing at my door looking gorgeous while I was standing here in sweat pants.

"Hi Candy!" She said as she walked in, giving me a bear hug. I about lost every ounce of vaginal secretions that my body possessed within that one moment. Her perky, round breast smashed into mine and her warm hands were planted firmly on my back. She was wearing a skirt and in my mind, I could feel the heat from her highly anticipated vagina. I hurriedly backed up from her because if I was going to pull this off, I had to keep my composure.

"Hey girl." I responded breathlessly.

"I know I'm early but I figured you could use a little help setting up."

"Aww! That's really sweet of you. Come on in and have a seat. I'm actually done with everything. I just have to go in here and put my clothes on." I led her to the living room and handed her the remote control to the stereo. I hurriedly went into my room and threw on the hot pink tube dress that I'd laid out to where. I loved that dress because I'd pulled many men while wearing it. But on this occasion, it was different because it was solely meant to grab the attention of a woman, whom if given the chance, I was going to turn out.

When the party started, I was nervous as hell. I didn't know if my scheme would work but I had to satisfy this urge or I was going to lose it. I sat anxiously as we played spades while drinking and bobbing our heads to the music. As the night progressed and people began to leave, I began to relax, Val and her husband left first, then one by one everybody started to head out. I kept Jenetta and Mario on the spade table because I knew that as long as they were there, Carolyn would be there. I made everyone drinks and as I tried to sneak the roofie in Carolyn's drink, Jenetta walked in the kitchen offering to help. I wanted to punch her in her face but I instead declined her offer and continued making drinks. And before

I knew it, this stupid heifer had picked up the drink I'd made for Carolyn and started drinking it. I literally wanted to slap the taste out of her mouth. Now I understood why very few people liked her because she was such a freaking idiot. I didn't have anymore roofies so now my plan to seduce Carolyn was all messed up. I would have to think of another way to get to Carolyn and as I walked back to the table I overheard Carolyn and Mario joking about smoking weed. That was my "Aha" moment because I had some California Love that my cousin had given to me and I knew its potency would knock Carolyn out just enough to where I could have my way with her.

Jenetta's dumb ass was on the couch passed out shortly after drinking my "special" drink and I simply let everyone think she had drunk too much. But I actually used Jenetta passing out to my advantage because I was able to convince Carolyn to stay over and help me with Jenetta. I pretty much tricked her into thinking I wanted to have a girl's night or should I say a *sleep* over.

After Mario left, Carolyn and I carried Jenetta to my spare bedroom and laid her on the bed. We put a trash can beside her in case she got sick and headed back to the living room. I poured Carolyn and I another strong drink and casually got my sack of chronic out and began rolling a blunt. Carolyn, who was in awe but cautious at the same time didn't know whether to smile or pretend that she didn't smoke. But before it was all over she and I were smoking, laughing and having a good time. And before I knew it, she was highly intoxicated and laid her head back on the couch and closed her eyes. My coochie immediately began to get wet as I imagined pushing up that tight black mini skirt she was wearing and putting my face in between her thighs. I was high, I was drunk and I was bold. I had confidence that I'd never had before but the closer I got to her, the more and more nervous I got. My hands began to shake and sweat began to pour down my brow. However, when her sweet scent hit my nose my body became overpowered by my desire to taste her. I first put her toes in my mouth and began to gently suck on them. Then I licked her legs and began moving my hand up between her thighs. She squirmed a little bit but she still didn't wake up. I gently pushed her skirt up and saw that she wasn't wearing any panties. At that moment my body went into the most explosive orgasm that I had ever experienced in my life. I took my finger and began gently rubbing her click. And as I kissed the inside of her thighs I heard her moan and that affirmed that she liked it. I made my way to her vagina that was so warm and gooey I wanted to submerge my face all in it. And as I took that first lick I felt her move. I looked up and saw her eyes opening. Her first glance was a groggy "where am I" look but the next one was a "what the fuck is going on" look. It was at that point that I knew I was in trouble.

Carolyn

"Damn, I'm messed up." I thought to myself as I laid my head back on Candy's couch. Candy and I had smoked a blunt of some potent weed and I was so blowed that all I could do was lay my head back and go to sleep. I started having a dream about me and Demarcus lying on the beach having sex. The dream was so vivid that I could actually *feel* him touching me, licking my feet, licking my legs and playing in my Juicy. It felt so good that I heard myself moan out loud. I quickly opened my eyes and looked around because I was hoping that nobody had heard me. And as I groggily opened my eyes I saw Candy in between my legs. I blinked because at that point I *knew* I had to have been dreaming. But as I became more alert and then saw the look of sheer terror in Candy's face I knew I wasn't dreaming. I was so in shock that I didn't know what to do. "Was this bitch really trying to have sex with me?" I thought to myself. I wiped my eyes one more time just to make sure that the weed wasn't making my mind play tricks on me. I took another quick survey of the room to make sure I wasn't crazy and I saw Jenetta's dumb ass standing in the doorway looking at me with the same type of shock that I was feeling. At that point all the alcohol and weed left my system and I went into kick ass mode. I didn't even give Candy time to speak before I jumped up and hit her ass with a two piece.

"Bitch what the hell is wrong with you? I ain't gay, are you crazy?" I screamed as I tried to beat her brains out. I couldn't believe what was going on. I was in shock but the shock didn't keep me from trying to kill her ass. Before I knew it, I'd picked the lamp up off the table and was about to bust her in the head with it until I felt an arm grab the lamp out of my hand. I whirled around to see Jenetta. I was about to swing on her until I heard her scream, "Carolyn no! You're going to kill her. Please stop. Please calm down." I blinked, took a deep breath and turned around. Candy was lying on the floor in a fetal position with hair and blood scattered all around her. Just looking at her made me want to start right back in on her ass but I knew if I did, I would in fact *kill* her. Instead, I chose to stand over her, spit on her ass and walk out the door.

Case #32487 Lost Innocence

Four year old Allissa awoke to the sound of music coming from the living room in her house. As she got out of bed, she tugged at her Hello Kitty pajamas and rubbed her big brown eyes. She pushed the door slightly ajar and peeked out to see what was going on. As usual it was another typical night of partying for her parents who were known for the hip and happening house parties that they threw at least three times a week. Her little stomach growled as she walked towards the kitchen. The air was thick with smoke and strong smells that she had smelled before but was unsure as to what they were. She did however recognize the familiar smell of alcohol.

Men and women stood all throughout the house. Some were dancing, some were talking and some were smoking and drinking. As she approached the kitchen the smell of fried chicken began to seep into her nostrils and overwhelm her famished little body. Her dad was leaning up against the counter smoking a really small white cigarette while her mom was frying chicken wings. When they saw Allissa, they yelled at her to go back to bed.

"But I'm hungry." She whined as she wrapped her long ponytail around her little fingers.

"Go back in your room now!" Her mom screamed. Crying, Allissa began to walk slowly back towards her room. On her way through the loud music and clouds of smoke her bladder led her to the bathroom. There was a young man standing in front of the door who smiled down at her. He appeared to be really nice and asked her, "You need some help little mama?"

"No, I just need to use the bathroom." She replied. A sly smile began to spread across his mouth as he again offered to help her. Becoming afraid she began to back away from the door while looking around for her mommy. He grabbed her arm and told her to be quiet. Tears started to roll down her face as he led her into the bathroom and shut the door behind her. He locked the door, put his hand over her mouth and pushed her to the floor. Allissa; paralyzed with fear, sat helplessly as he forcefully spread her legs and pulled down her "Hello Kitty" pajama pants. She couldn't scream nor could she move and when her private parts began to experience an excruciating pain that she'd never felt before, she blacked out.

The next morning when she woke up in her bed she thought that it had all been a dream until she tried to sit up and felt the sharp pains that ran through her little legs, stomach and now violated private part.

"Mommy." She cried out.

"Mommy. I hurt really bad. I really hurt mommy." She cried out again to no response. She waited a few seconds and then called out to her parents again, "Mommy, Daddy. Mommy, Daddy." When she still didn't get a response, she figured that her parents were still sleeping in like they usually did when they had had one of their parties. She knew that trying to wake them up wouldn't work because they usually were sleeping so hard that she couldn't wake them up. On more than one occasion after unsuccessfully trying to wake her parents after a party, the four year old had had to get herself ready for the Head Start bus that was usually there by 8:00 am. And she knew that today would be one of those days. She really didn't want to go to school but she was afraid that the mean man was still somewhere in the house and would kill her and her parents if she didn't get out of the house.

Although she was in terrible pain, she forced herself up out of bed and limped to the bathroom. She froze immediately when she approached the bathroom door. Memories of the brutal attack flooded her memory and as she stood stoically in front of the door; she began urinating on herself. She screamed because of how bad her private part burned when she peed. Fear overwhelmed her because she didn't know if the mean man was still around. At that point she knew that she could never go into that bathroom or any bathroom ever again.

She slowly backed away from the door and made her way into the kitchen. She pulled a chair up to the sink and splashed water onto her face and swished water around in her mouth. She then slowly walked back into her bedroom and began putting on her clothes. After she was dressed she limped painstakingly towards the front door where she saw several people laying on the couch and floor sleeping or snoring loudly. She got her backpack out of the living room closet and headed out to the front porch to wait for the bus.

The bumpy bus ride to school was almost unbearable for her to endure because of the shooting pains that were surging throughout her lower body. None of her classmates wanted to sit beside her on the bus because they said she smelled like pee. The bus monitor was too busy to notice because she was dealing with Billy Roberts who cried every morning on the way to school. Plus they were used to her coming to school unkempt or smelly anyway because they were very familiar with her parent's parties. After she arrived at school she walked slowly into the building. Somehow she made it to her classroom where she hung her backpack in her cubby and headed to her seat. She sat quietly with all kinds of thoughts going through her small brain. What had happened to her? Why did she hurt so badly? Why hadn't her parents rescued her? Why had the nice man wanted to hurt her so bad? Was she going to be pregnant because wasn't that what happened when a boy got on top of you? At least that's what she'd heard Lilly Jackson tell Minda Lewis while they were all in the sandbox.

The events from the previous night consumed her. The things that the nice man had done to her hadn't been so nice. She remembered the mean look he had in his eyes. She remembered the floor being cold against her back as he'd climbed his large and overpowering body on top of her. She remembered how he seemed like a giant with such foul breath that it had almost made her vomit. She would never forget that smell, but more than anything; she would never forget the pain.

A cold chill ran down her spine and she shivered. She had an overwhelming desire to cry. She wanted to get up and jump into her favorite teacher; Mrs. Gilliam's arms so that she could console her. But she remembered the man saying that he would kill her if she ever told their secret. She looked around the classroom at her peers. She saw mouths moving but she didn't hear any sounds. She was too encompassed within her own thoughts. She wondered if they could look at her and see what had happened. She could still smell the strong stench of pee on herself but she didn't care because no one would come around her and maybe if she had smelled like pee last night then the man wouldn't have hurt her.

"Allissa, did you hear what I said?" She snapped back into reality and looked at her teacher. She'd barely heard anything that was going on in her classroom. Her stomach growled because she was still hungry from the previous night so when her teacher handed her a muffin and carton of milk she gobbled it down like there was no tomorrow. When station time came, she struggled to get up and walk to her station. As she got up, she didn't notice the smears of blood that she'd left behind in her seat. However, her teacher, Mrs. Gilliam did. She also noticed how slowly Allissa walked as she went over to her station.

Mrs. Gilliam walked over to Allissa and whispered, "Allissa, what happened? Why are you bleeding? Why are you walking like that?"

Allissa wanted to answer her but fear stalled any words from coming out of her mouth. She wanted to cry, she wanted to scream; not only because of the severe pain, but because of the overwhelming sadness that she felt. She felt violated, she felt ashamed and she felt betrayed because grownups were supposed to protect children, not hurt them. She stood there froze, unable to move or respond. She was confused because she didn't really know what had happened to her. Ms. Gilliam reached down to pick her up but Allissa backed away from her because she suddenly had a strong distrust for grownups. Ms. Gilliam noticed Allissa's response and didn't waste any time trying to process it with her. She picked

Allissa up, who began screaming to the top of her lungs and carried her to the nurse's office. She then alerted the Director who called 9-1-1. Allissa was rushed to the hospital and since no one could reach her parents, Ms. Gilliam went with her. The doctor examined her and then began talking with Ms. Gilliam. They talked quietly on the other side of the curtain but Allissa was able to hear some of the things they were saying. The main thing that caught her attention was the word "raped".

"Hmm, I wonder what "raped" means?" She thought to herself as she fell into a deep sleep.

Carolyn Black

"Fosterberg County Department of Social Services, this is Carolyn Black. How may I assist you?"

"Hello Ms. Black. My name is Lolita Hollingsworth and I'm a nurse at Fosterberg Memorial Hospital. We have a little four year old girl here who has been raped and as a result has been severely damaged. We've been trying to reach her parents but no one is answering so we sent the police over to her house. The teacher has told me that the child has come to school on several occasions unkempt but it wasn't anything that was deemed necessary to report until now. The little girl is severely traumatized and will not speak. She screams and fights if you come near her. She's going to be here for a long time due to the severity of her injuries but we are unsure as to how this happened and if her home environment is safe for her to return to." I sighed. "Ok. I'm on my way."

I hung up the phone and stood up to get my things together. I really wasn't in the mind set to go and tend to this child because I still couldn't get the shit that happened between me and Candy out of my head. I looked down at my hands and saw all the scratches and bruises from where I'd tried to punch a hole through her head. The nerve of that bitch to try and get me tore up so she could basically *rape me*. I just couldn't understand where it all came from. She was cool as hell and I thought things would be smooth between us unlike me and Zian or me and Jenetta. But hell who knew that the heifer was going to try to take my Juicy. That shit had come out of nowhere. What was wrong with her? Was she crazy? I was glad that I had beat the shit out of her and I thought to myself "she better not show her face up in here today or I'ma beat dat ass again."

"Humph." I mumbled out loud without realizing it as I slung my purse and the strap of my brief case across my shoulder.

"Carolyn, I need to see you in my office, NOW!" Valerie shouted impetuously from her office door. She sounded pissed but I really wasn't in the mood to hear any bullshit today so I all but stomped into her office and shut the door. "Yes, what is it?" I asked impatiently. I knew I was testing the waters but at that point I didn't give a crap.

"I'm going to need you to check your attitude and leave that shit outside the door." She said as she put me in check; letting me know who was boss. I stood there coyly feeling very subordinate.

"As of now you are suspended. I want you to go in your office, pack your shit and leave here not to return for one month." She stood up, marched to her calendar and calculated the date for my return.

"You can return on Thursday, May 25. Now you're dismissed." She stated bluntly without blinking or missing a beat. I didn't think I was hearing her right so I responded by saying,

"Valerie, what the hell are you talking about? How am I suspended? What have I done to get suspended?"

"Carolyn, do you think I'm crazy? Did you think I wouldn't find out about what happened between you and Candy? Huh? Do you really think that shit wouldn't have come back to me?" I shook my head and thought to myself, "that damn Jenetta."

"Well honestly I wasn't concerned about that because that I didn't do anything wrong." I replied candidly.

"Carolyn, you never do anything wrong but I be damn if your ass ain't always in the midst of something. First it was Zian and now its Candy and hell it's always been Jenetta. I don't know what your problem is with women. It's like you can't stand for somebody to come in and shine just as bright as you. I'm sick of this shit Carolyn.

That's two damn social workers that I'm going to have to replace because of your ornery ass. You think your shit don't stink Carolyn and yes I agree that you're a great social worker but damnit there are others out there that care about children just as much as you do but without that shitty ass attitude you have." I cut her off because at that point I had become livid. My pet peeve was for people to try and pin me as being conceded because I've always gone out of my way to be as humble as possible.

"First of all Valerie, is it my fault that the one unmarried man that I was kicking it with just happened to be Zian's fiancé? Did *you* even know who he was? No you didn't. Second of all, that fucking bitch Candy tried to drug me and seduce me. So what the hell, *your highness*, did *I* have to do with that? How did I cause that? You are supposed to be my friend, on my side, so how can you even stand here and talk to me like I'm some random worker who you haven't known for years. If you want to know the truth about it, I think these heifers are jealous of me. And you and I both know that I'm not conceited so why the hell would I be concerned about somebody stealing my shine when I'm confident in knowing that my freaking shine is all mine!" I said with as much attitude and cockiness that I could conjure up.

She stepped forward, stuck her pointer finger out and retorted; "Now you listen here heifer! If I wasn't your friend I wouldn't be doing this. If your black ass wasn't so stuck on yourself and so damn bull headed then you would see that. What do you think the director is going to say when she finds out that we are going to have to replace another social worker on your account? Then don't you think that's going to lead to an investigation which is then going to lead to a...," she dropped her voice to a whisper, "drug... test? Now if you don't get the fuck out of here, I'm going to let them fire your ass." She concluded with finality.

Pissed because I knew she was right, I jerked my shit up and yanked the door open prepared to slam it so hard that it would break into pieces. But just as I was about to release the door, I remembered that precious little girl who was at the hospital waiting for someone to come and rescue her. So I stopped in my tracks and turned around.

"Somebody needs to go to Fosterberg Memorial for this case." I took out the notes I'd jotted down earlier and tossed them onto her desk. I turned around and stormed out the door. Of course everybody and their mama was standing in the office and lobby being nosy but I didn't give a crap. I felt betrayed. How was I the one getting suspended and not Candy when she was the damn perpetrator? I was so pissed that I started to get into my car, drive to her house and beat her up again. What was I going to do for a month without a job? I mean I wasn't concerned about money because I knew that I had a rainy day stash plus I knew my *tricks* would come through for me if necessary. It was more so that my pride was hurt. I'd never even been written up at a job before, much less suspended.

I slammed the door to my 2011 Honda Accord and put my head on the steering wheel. I wanted to cry so badly but I was so pissed that I didn't want to give any of those mofos the pleasure of being able to break me because damnit, I'm unbreakable. I took a deep breath, sucked it up and cranked my car up. As I was pulling out of the parking lot, I started to head home but thought otherwise. I looked in the rearview mirror and said to myself, "I'm gonna get you high today. You're suspended, you ain't got no job and you don't have shit to do." Then I busted out laughing at my rendition of "Smoky" from the movie "Friday." My little joke made me feel better and although I really didn't know what I was going to be doing for a whole month, I knew one thing I wasn't going to do; and that was sit around and wallow in sorrow. I called my cousin Brandon to see what he was doing. I knew that he had a very flexible job and probably had nothing to do either. I figured that we could do nothing together and get high in the mean time.

Of course he told me to come through which I gladly did. We smoked, laughed, talked and caught up. Brandon was my favorite aunt Glenda's son and we'd always been close because we were only a few months apart. Aunt Glenda's family owned a string of restaurants that specialized in American and Dominican foods. She also owned several hair salons and barbershops so needless to say they weren't hurting for money. Brandon, who had a degree in business, managed the hair salons and barber shops. He did a great job and had things set up to where he worked when he wanted to. In the meantime, his *side job* also profited because he interacted with so many different kinds of people. I loved Brandon because we always had a good time together and he always made me laugh.

After listening to his crazy stories about women, the local gossip (because he knew it all) and things going on with the family, we decided to go get a drink. Knowing that I couldn't be seen at Jar Bar, we decided to head on the east side of town where I knew I wouldn't run into anybody I worked with because the eastside was THE GHETTO. But Brandon and I grew up around that area so we weren't pressed or concerned. We had a lot of respect on that side of town because we had such a large family and everybody at least knew one of us. Plus neither Brandon nor I was afraid to open up a can whoop ass if we had to.

We pulled in at a place called Buster's. It was what I called a legalized "Juke Joint" because it was a hole in the wall type place that served cheap liquor, had the best fish sandwiches in town and featured homemade live music that ranged from the Blues to Jazz to R&B. Anybody from off the street that could play an instrument or sing was allowed to come in there and perform. Nevertheless I loved the place and had had some of the best times in my life there.

After we went in, we ordered drinks and sat back and listened to Loretta Thomas from 25th street who was singing the blues. I giggled to myself as I thought about Loretta and the quintessential ideology. Catching on to why I was giggling, Brandon started laughing too. Both of us were high and before we knew it we were laughing so hard that we were both doubled over in pain. Once we'd regained our composure we ordered fish sandwiches and fries. We also ordered beer and few shots of vodka. We drank, laughed and enjoyed the music. Soon thereafter, my very beer filled bladder got the best of me so I got up and headed towards the bathroom. I went in, handled my business and washed my hands. I looked in the mirror, touched up my makeup and headed back to the table. By that time Benny, Marshall and Junior (also from 25th

street) had joined Loretta Thomas and were now singing some song that they'd made up. As I listened to the song, I realized that it was actually a nice song. It was one those backwoods thumpin' bumpin' kind of songs where you patted your feet and snapped your fingers. Loretta threw her head back and belted out the words:

I wanted to let you goooooooooooo
I wanted to let you gooooooooo
And I don't know why I held on so long

I thought you were the one for me.
I did what I thought I should to make us be.
But what happened? I end up hurting me...
I was on a roller coaster and sometimes I couldn't breathe
But that's over now and baby I am free.
So release your hold from me, there is no more we.
You are outta here because God is directing me....

I wanted to let you goooooooooooo
I wanted to let you gooooooooo
And I don't know why I held ooooooon soooo long

I bobbed my head as I walked through the crowded maze of tables and people who were up rocking to the beats of the song. Everybody was feeling it because it spoke to everybody in the room in some kind of way; whether it was a relationship gone wrong, hard times, drug use or whatever else. I on the other hand was high so of course I was in analytical mode and my analysis of the song made me think about the situation with my job, my relationships with men and the overwhelming sadness that came over me sometimes. As I was walking, beginning to feel empowered by the song, I came through a clearing within only a few feet of my table when I happened to look to the left and saw Demarcus leaned up against the bar. My heart started pounding so hard that I thought it would burst out of my chest and all the logic that the song had been speaking to me stopped talking. My hands began to sweat and I could barely breathe. He looked so good in his fitted dark Levis, brown Polo boots and white Polo shirt. I tried to turn away before he saw me and as I was walking off, I damn near tripped over a chair and broke my neck. I was so embarrassed because when I looked up he looked right at me and smiled. He motioned for me to come over there but I was so embarrassed that I didn't want to walk over to him. Eventually his gravitational pull overpowered me so I turned and told my cousin I was going to the bar to grab a drink. Turning away from Demarcus to talk to my cousin bought me some time to get myself together. I smoothed out my clothes and sashayed over to where he was. We embraced and the smell of his cologne overwhelmed me. I had missed him so much and all I wanted to do was get him back to my place so he could get me high and drunk and then take advantage of me.

"So, long time, no see Ms. Black. What can I get you to drink?" He asked while looking me straight in my eyes without even as much as a blink. He took my hand and began intertwining his fingers within mine. I blushed and was immediately pissed at myself for letting him see me blushing. It had been weeks since he'd called me and I didn't want him to see me sweat. I didn't want him to know how much I'd missed him. But nevertheless my feelings for him were written all over my face and wouldn't let me hide. I wanted to be inside his strong arms but the fight in me kicked in and I snatched my hand away from him.

"I'll take a patron on the rocks." I replied coolly. He laughed because he knew what I was doing. He ordered the drink and sat it down in front of me. He scooted his bar stool back away from me and said, "Ok so does this make you feel better? I mean why you being so cold Carolyn?" He said through giggles. I hated it when he mocked me but soon I was giggling to.

"Screw you Demarcus. You know I don't like not hearing from you. You usually hit me up at least twice a week." I replied jokingly trying not to sound as desperate as I was feeling.

"Baby you know how ole girl is. She been on me lately." The mention of *her* made a ball of anger begin to burn in my stomach. I took a deep breath and started counting to ten as I watched his lips move without even hearing what he was saying. I knew that she was his wife legally but at the same time I felt like I was his true love and the person he was supposed to be with. It was supposed to be me lying down with him at night, cooking his dinners and rubbing his feet. Hell I knew that heifer didn't do any of those things because the bitch couldn't boil water and she sure in the hell wasn't going to ruin her Lee Press on Nails to rub his feet.

"Carolyn? You alright? You checked out on me for a minute." I blinked and regained my composure. I realized that my body was tense and my hands were tightened into fists. At that moment I realized that I needed to get up and leave. My emotions were in control and I wasn't. I kept telling myself time after time again that I was going to leave Demarcus alone because he was dangerous. He made me feel things that I shouldn't have been feeling for any man, especially a married one. I had built a brick wall around my heart a long time ago and I'd be damned if any man, especially Demarcus was going to bust through it. I am a smart woman and I know that Demarcus would truly never be mine therefore I was setting myself up for failure. I took my shot of patron to the face and started to get up.

"Demarcus, listen, I don't think we should see each other anymore. I mean I can't do this married thing with you anymore because I'm falling for you and you are tied to someone else. I wish you the best." I said as I started walking away from the bar. He grabbed my arm and pulled me to him. He kissed me and said, "Now Carolyn, do you think you gonna walk away from me just like that?" He was so close to me that I could smell the Michelob Ultra on his breath.

I jerked my arm away from him and turned to walk away. Just as I was about to take a step, I looked up and was blinded by a mass of fire engine red hair. It was her, Demarcus' wife. She stood with her hands on her hips and a glare so fierce that it about matched her hair. Now I was a little tipsy and coming down from my high but the sight of her sobered me up quickly. I sized her up and eased into my fighter's stance because I knew that she might try to get bad. She was shorter than me but I could tell that she could throw down with the best of em' and by the way she made the majority of her movements with her left arm, I knew that she was left handed. She was hood as hell so I knew that she probably had a blade on her somewhere but I wasn't about to let that bitch even think about getting that close to me.

Although Demarcus was her husband, I was heated all the same. I knew it was crazy but all I could think about was the nerve of this bitch to look at me like she wanted do something. And although I was ready to tear her head off, the social worker and counselor in me rationalized her point for just a second in my mind because I knew that if I was married to a man like Demarcus I would be ready to devour any bitch that so much as looked at him the wrong way. But the true Carolyn Black mixed with the patron in me wasn't about to let this bitch put her hands on me so I waited calmly and patiently for her to make her move.

"Demarcus, who the hell is this bitch? And what the hell are you doing all up in her face like she me." She spat out with an emphasis on *she* and *me.* My blood began to boil but I kept my cool. In my peripheral vision I saw Demarcus nervously shifting from side to side.

"Answer me!" She screamed causing a few of the other patrons to begin taking notice.

"Charmanita chill out. You tripping." Demarcus said coolly.

Charmanita? I thought to myself. What kind of name is that? But then this was a hood rat so of course the name fit the face.

I waited for his response. I wanted him to curse her out and tell her that he loved me and didn't want to be with her anymore. My heart yearned for it because in my mind I was thinking that our dirty little secret was out now and Demarcus would profess his love for me.

"Chill out? Chill out mutherfucker? You got some bourgeois ass white looking bitch up in your face and you telling me to chill? Is this the bitch that you been sneaking around with? Huh? Huh?"

"I'm not going to be too many more of your bitches." I

replied looking her right in her face in order to ensure that she understood exactly what I meant.

"And what the fuck you gonna do?"

"Demarcus, you betta get your wife before I hurt her." I said. My tone was so low and so serious that I almost scared myself. I didn't like going to the dark place that this broad was taking me to but she was asking for it.

"Charmanita, I told you to calm the fuck down. Now let's go. You ain't getting ready to cause no drama up in here and embarrass me."

"Oh, for real Demarcus. You taking this bitch's side?"She asked while rolling her neck. But before she could get *bitch* out of her mouth good, I hit her in her mouth so hard that whatever words she wanted to say next went right back down her throat. And out of nowhere I felt two strong hands grab me and lift me up. It wasn't until I was flying mid air to the ground that I realized that it had been Demarcus who had picked me up and threw me on the ground. I was so stunned that all I could do was sit on the ground and look up at him in sheer confusion.

"Charmanita, I don't even know this chick. She was flirting with me after I was nice and brought her a drink. This trick knew I was married." Seeing his mouth move but not totally comprehending the words that were coming out, I couldn't believe that the person I was looking at was Demarcus. He looked at me like I was gutter trash and didn't acknowledge me at all. All the things we'd done together, all the kinky, passionate sex we'd had and all the conversations suddenly seemed to flash before my eyes and then obliterate into the fire red hair of this hood rat bitch that was holding her mouth trying to catch the blood that was dripping off her lips. Rage began to overcome me and right as I was about to pounce on Demarcus I saw Brandon flying through the air like he was superman with his fist aimed at Demarcus' face. He hit Demarcus with such force that he went flying back into the bar. I then took my opportunity to take all frustrations out on his ass with my fist. And as I was socking him with all my might, I saw fire red hair in my peripheral vision. As I turned to my left, this bitch actually landed a blow to my jaw. It was at the point that I blacked out. The last thing I remember saying was, "Bitch you got me fucked up! I will set it off in this mutherfucker!" And that I did.

When I came to, Brandon was rushing me to the car before the police arrived. He threw me in the front seat kicking and screaming but eventually I calmed down. I was silent the rest of the way home because I was trying to process what had just happened. I was hurt, I was ashamed and more than anything, I was embarrassed because I had got played like a trumpet in front of that raggedy bitch like I was nothing. When Brandon dropped me off, I rolled the fattest blunt I could get my hands on. I went into the living room and slide down the wall and cried my eyes out as I smoked. I just couldn't believe how Demarcus had done me. I tried to pull myself together but this had been the day from hell for me and I couldn't fight my emotions anymore. I cried until I started hyperventilating. And at the point when I was weak from crying, my phone rang. Secretly hoping it was Demarcus calling to beg my forgiveness I answered it without even seeing who it was.

"Hello?" I snapped.

"Carolyn...baby what's wrong?" It was my mother and at the sweet sound of her voice I broke down. Before I knew it, she was knocking at my door and I was spilling my guts to her.

Case #32488 I Tried Him and I Know Him

After my mother left last night, I felt so relieved. Here I was; suspended from work without pay for a whole month, betrayed by Demarcus for his trifling ass wife and I was the cause of another co-worker having to get transferred, although I didn't feel bad about that part at all. I mean hell; Candy got what she deserved, trying to drug and rape me. I'd beat the shit out of that heifer and I would do it again if I ever saw her out in the streets. And of course there was Jenetta's bitch ass. She was on the top of my hit list for her part in this mess but I knew that I was skating on thin ice so I would never be able to unleash the physical beating I wanted to give her due to all the crap I was in; but nevertheless, I would get her.

I shook my head because I knew that I had no business plotting on Jenetta when I was already in a heap of trouble but I just couldn't help but wonder why these things kept happening to me and what I had done to make people feel some type of way about me. As I got out of bed to make myself some coffee, I leaned against the counter and reflected back on my life. My childhood and young adult life had been ok minus the bullshit I had endured at the hands of men and jealous women. I worked my butt off to get my degree and I landed a job that I really love. Based off these things I feel like I should be a really happy person but my personal life has been so shitty that it overshadows all the other accomplishments I've made in my life. I am a woman who constantly walks in duplicity; wearing the same face with different personalities. I try to keep the two separated but my personal life has made me bitter and shameless. I lash out at anyone who makes me feel threatened whether it's a man, a coworker, a client or just a regular person in the street. I screw married men and honestly, I don't give a shit. Or I should say that I didn't give a shit until I saw the look on my mother's face when I told her about the things I had been doing. She was a mirror for me and she forced me to look at myself. I realized that I was a broken, angry and bloodthirsty woman out to get revenge on all the people; men and women, who had hurt me. And throughout my vengeful rampage, I didn't give a damn about who I hurt or how often I hurt them as long as I was immune to the pain.

No one except Val knew about my double life and it had been really hard maintaining all those secrets. But when I revealed everything to my mom and she listened without judging me, it was like a ton of bricks had been lifted off my chest. The way she had laid there with me with her petite arms wrapped around me like I was an infant made it all better. She gave me the strength I needed to move on because for so long I had been hiding my lifestyle from my parents and I was tired of the lies and the pretending. I wanted to be free and talking to my mom had liberated me. I hated it so badly when she left to go home because I wanted her to stay and sleep in the bed with me like she used to when I was little. Now that she was gone, I felt lighter but the pain was still there. I couldn't get Demarcus off my mind. The way he'd turned his back on me after all we'd been through, had put me back in that same place of vulnerability that I'd sworn off years ago.

I wanted to eat but thinking of Demarcus ruined my appetite and reopened the flood gates. Massive waves of tears began to roll down face. My heart ached and burned as I reminisced about how cold and cruel he was to me. He'd looked at me like I was trash not like the woman whom he'd spent countless days and nights professing his love to. Not like the woman who rubbed his feet, cooked his food and made love to him like I knew no other woman could. I knew everything he wanted and I knew everything he needed. I knew how to make him smile, I knew how to make him laugh and I knew how to soothe the anguish that the hood rat wife often bestowed upon him. But the most gut wrenching thing of all was that he reciprocated all those same things. He knew me inside and out, from top to bottom. I felt no shame when I was with him and my double mask was nonexistent because when I was around him I was just Carolyn. Not Carolyn the social worker or Carolyn the mistress, I was simply Carolyn the woman. I just didn't understand how or why he could treat me like I was nothing, like I was...a stranger. My heart ached so intensely that I had to grab onto the edge of the counter and double over in order to keep myself from hyperventilating. I didn't think I would ever be able to breathe again. But as I cried and forced myself to breathe, I realized that there was one good thing that had been revived through the pain and vulnerability that I was feeling; I started to feel alive again. My body, that had been cold for so long, slowly began to feel warm again. Those dormant emotions that I thought were nonexistent were still there and had ignited a strong revelation within me. I now know that if I can feel genuine pain then there is a strong possibility that I will also have the opportunity to feel joy and happiness.

The thought of happiness perked me up and the overwhelming sensation of hyperventilating began to cease. My strength was renewed and I decided that I would eat. I cooked an egg, a piece of sausage and toasted an English muffin. When I took that first bite it seemed to have a whole new taste. It was the taste of liberation and freedom. After I finished eating, I decided to clean my house from top to bottom. I walked over to my CD player and put in an old Reverend Milton Brunson and The Thompson Community Choir Singers CD and pushed play. My favorite song, *I Tried Him and I Know Him* began to play. As the singer began singing the song, it was if she was staring into my soul and singing to and about me. I closed my eyes and simply leaned up against the wall. I welcomed the tears that began to fall because although I knew my life was a mess, I now had a new outlook on figuring out how to fix it.

Willie Black

Willie Black barely slept a wink after she'd arrived home from Carolyn's house. She had really wanted to stay with her daughter and make all her "boo boos" go away but she knew that she had to let Carolyn be a woman and deal with her problems herself. It had hurt her so bad to hear the things that her precious daughter had been doing with married men but she dared not scold her when she was already in so much pain. She knew Carolyn was smart and she was still very proud of her baby despite the things she'd done. Although she and Carolyn's father, Ricardo, had put Carolyn up on a pedestal her whole life they both had known that she was not perfect. Nobody was; but nevertheless they'd still looked at Carolyn as their princess. When Willie woke up the next morning, she was dog tired and felt terrible. Her body felt like it had been buried under a pile of bricks; but she figured it was because she'd tossed and turned all night worrying about her Carolyn. She was concerned about her daughter's reputation and her job and that temper that Carolyn had inherited from her grandmother. It took every ounce of strength she had to roll over, kiss her sleeping husband on the cheek and get out of bed. As she walked into the kitchen to fix Ricardo's lunch box for the day and prepare his coffee and breakfast, her arm began to feel numb and her chest began to fill like it was caving in. She took a deep breath and sat down at the table to get herself together. She thought about Carolyn again and knew that she would never breathe a word to anyone about what they had discussed. After all Carolyn had really opened up to her and she knew that that had been a difficult thing for her picture perfect daughter to do. As she regained her composure, she smiled and thought about how blessed she was to have the family that she had; a great husband, beautiful children and financial security. What more could she ask for? She began to hum one of her favorite hymns; *He's Always Looking Out for Me,* as she made a turkey sandwich to put into Ricardo's lunch box. But with each move that she made, her chest got heavier and her arm became less functional. She then began having trouble breathing.

She turned to walk towards the bedroom to wake Ricardo but before she could make it across the threshold, she fell to the ground.

Carolyn Black

I was really working up a sweat as I cleaned my house. I had cleaned the living room and the kitchen from top to bottom, and was now working on cleaning my bathrooms. I was really grooving to my Rev. Milton Brunson CD and loving how it was helping all my problems to melt away. I finished up the bathroom and started on my disaster of a bedroom when my phone rang. Thinking to myself, this is probably Demarcus calling to beg me back, I ignored it and kept going. I didn't want to talk to anyone on the phone because I really needed this time to clear my head but when it rang a second and third time, I suspected that it was something important so I answered it.

"Hello?" I answered in an irritated voice.

"Hmmm, you always got some kind of attitude don't you?" My older sister Sylvia said into the phone.

Although the sound of her voice annoyed me even more, I didn't want to let this heifer ruin my good mood. I didn't know why the hussy was calling me in the first place so in the most sarcastic tone that I could conjure up; I replied, "Yes Sylvia, what can I do for you my dear sister. I mean if you're calling me, than it most definitely must be something of great importance."

"Well, you smart ass, high yeller heifer, I was just calling to tell you that your mama had a heart attack and is in the hospital." All the sarcasm that I had conjured up for my sister descended to my throat and stopped there. I felt like I was being choked. My ability to speak was halted and all I could do was hold the phone and stare into space as the words "your mom had a heart attack" began to register in my brain. How could that be? I had just seen her; she was just here last night. My heart began pounding in my ears and I thought for a second that if I didn't breathe then I would pass out.

"Are you still there? Did you hear what I said?" Sylvia

barked out.

Still struggling to regain my speech; all I could manage to push out of my mouth was, "Y-Yeah. Where?"

"She's at Baptist Memorial Hospital in the ER. They're getting ready to take her into surgery."

I don't even know if I hung the phone up before I was grabbing my purse and running towards the door. As I opened it, Mario was standing there with his arm up as if he was preparing to knock. I had no idea what the hell he was doing there, nor did I care because I had to get to my mama. When he saw the look of terror and desperation on my face he immediately went into rescue mode.

"Carolyn, what's wrong? What's going on?" I couldn't answer his questions because my mind was no longer in control. I was being navigated by my feet.

He gently grabbed me by my arm and said, "Carolyn, you don't even have any shoes on. Please, tell me what's going on." My reflexes were telling me to knock the shit out of him and keep going but the one ounce of rationality that I had left in my head allowed me to say, "My mom had a heart attack." Again going into rescue mode, Mario grabbed my keys out of my hand, ran in the house and grabbed the first pair of shoes he saw and ran back to the car. He got in the driver's seat and drove me to the hospital. I don't remember talking to him; I don't even remember the drive to the hospital. All I could think about was how my mom had just been there last night and how I knew that I would not be able to survive if something happened to her.

When we arrived at the hospital, I saw my sisters and brother sitting in the waiting room, huddled up together. My father was standing up against the wall staring off into space. My father was a very strong man and did not display his emotions openly and although he was trying to put up a front, I knew that he was a wreck just like the rest of us. When he saw me, he reached out his arms like I was a ten year old running to her daddy after he'd just come home from work. And like that ten year old I ran into his arms and buried my head in his shoulder. I, like him was very good at masking my feelings but all of that went out the window.

"Daddy, how is she?"

Refusing to look in my eyes, he replied, "She's not doing to good Curly. They are going to have to do open heart surgery on her. She has to have an emergency double heart valve replacement surgery. They are prepping her right now." Stunned, I kind of just backed up from him and looked around. There were a few people scattered here and there in the waiting room and nurses and doctors walking around. It was as if I was having an out of body experience and although there were a lot of things going on around me, all I could hear was...silence. My dad's lips were moving but I couldn't hear him. Mario's lips were moving but I couldn't hear him either. It was, however the snide comment, "It's about time she got here," that resonated in my ears. And as if I was watching myself in a movie in slow motion, before I knew it, I was flying through the air towards my sister with my hands stretched out to choke the life out of her. Her eyes bulged out of her head with fear; I'm assuming from the surprise of my attack and the look I probably had on my face. But before I could get her, my little brother John sideswiped me and caught me midair. I looked at both my sisters; who I knew hated me, in their eyes and with the sound of Satan in my voice I said, "My mother is in the hospital and if either one of y'all bitches disrespect that or me again, I will claw your damn eyeballs out. This ain't neither the place nor the time. If you got something you want to say to me, we can handle that when I know that my mama is ok."

I was so emotional and angry that I was foaming at the mouth and as I talked little drips of spittle landed on their faces. They didn't try me because they knew they would be fighting a losing battle. My brother, who was holding onto me tried to take me outside but I yanked away from him and walked down the hall so I could catch my breath. I had to calm myself down and then I realized that it wasn't my sisters that I was angry at. My body was simply going crazy. My central nervous system was on the verge of shutting down, my fight or flight system was in overdrive and my emotions were off the Rector Scale. I leaned up against the wall and cried.

"Carolyn, the doctor is here to talk to you all about your mother." Mario said as he handed me a tissue and put his arm around me. The doctor informed us that the surgery would take up to seven hours and he assured us that he would have the nurse contact us periodically to give us an update. He led us into a family waiting room by which no one else was there due to it being solely for families in this type of predicament. There was a TV, three couches, a table, a vending machine and some chairs. There was a large window facing downtown Winston-Salem and a small desk that held a telephone and a bible. My dad and brother sat on one couch, my sisters on another and Mario and I sat on the remaining couch. The room was silent with the exception of announcements being made over the intercom, people walking down the hallways and the TV which was on a station that no one was paying attention to. Just when I began feeling claustrophobic and thought I couldn't take it anymore, Brandon walked through the door. I wanted to jump up and tackle him and squeeze him to death but I had to remain composed. So I got up, hugged him and introduced him to Mario. After he'd gone around and hugged the rest of my family, he asked me if I wanted to step outside. At that point I declined because Mario was there and I wasn't sure if I could let him in on my marijuana smoking. My dad was also unaware but I didn't give two shits if my sisters knew.

My cousin Brandon was the breath of fresh air that we all needed. We all loved Brandon equally and he was very neutral. We began talking about silly things going on in his life and how his baby mama was stalking him. Before we knew it, we were all laughing and loosening up. The doctor's called and gave us an update about mom. They reported that she was doing ok and the surgery was going well. Afterwords, I went to use the bathroom and once I looked at myself in the mirror I was appalled by what I saw. My hair was in a bushy ponytail, I had on old raggedy sweat pants and a Winston-Salem State t-shirt that I had had since I was a freshman. My hands and body were ashy from cleaning my house and scrubbing the floors and I realized that I hadn't showered or brushed my teeth. I would have been embarrassed under any other circumstances but in this case I didn't care. However I did go to the nurses' station to get a travel tooth brush and tooth paste. I washed my face, brushed my teeth, and washed under my arms. Luckily, my mom had always taught me to carry deodorant and lotion in my purse so I was able to decrease the funk and ashiness that I had going on. I pulled out my comb and smoothed my ponytail down the best I could and put on some chap stick so my lips wouldn't look like a cracked bar of soap. When I arrived back in the waiting room with my family, I was relieved when Mario informed that he had to go home to handle some business and would be back later because I knew this was my window of time to go and get blowed with Brandon.

I told my father that Brandon and I were going for a walk and we would return soon. However, my father, being the clever man that he was invited himself to tag along. My sisters and brother also decided that they needed some fresh air since we had already gotten a call from the doctor giving us an update on mom's status. We gave the nurse my dad's cell phone number in case anything went wrong while we were outside the hospital. I rolled my eyes towards Brandon who let out a giggle. I was pissed because having my family tag along meant no reefer for me. However; my father being the prim, proper Christian man that he was busted my bubble.

"Um, Carolyn and Brandon, y'all think I'm crazy but I wasn't born yesterday. I know what y'all was coming out here to do." Trying to play it off, I looked at my dad like I had no idea what he was talking about.

"Daddy, what are you talking about? I just needed some fresh air."

"I *bet* you needed some *fresh air*. Hell I ain't mad at ya. We all need some *fresh air* and in this situation I think we should all get in the jeep and share some fresh air." My dad said with a serious face. My eyes bulged out of my head as I looked at Brandon and my sisters who were also in shock.

"I know y'all kids smoke reefer. I ain't crazy. Shoot I smoke me a little bit here and there myself. Hell, your mama smokes with me." He said with a chuckle. Us kids all looked at each other in bewilderment at the thought of our parents smoking marijuana. And although my dad had admitted it, I still didn't know how to feel about smoking it with him. Hell, I was even more blown away by the fact that my stuck up ass sisters smoked weed. Me and my brother John got high together all the time so I knew he smoked and Brandon was my supplier so of course we'd smoked together.

"Well Brandon, what's it going to be? We smoking or not? " My dad asked, trying to be cool, with a quick smile. I had to choke back my laughter because my dad was really blowing my mind.

"Shit y'all grown now so we ain't got to hide nothing from each other. Just don't tell your mama." And with that being said, none of us could no longer hold it in; we just burst out laughing. We then loaded up in Brandon's Yukon Denali and smoked it out. I was in awe because when I turned to my left, my sisters were hitting the blunt and when I looked ahead; my dad was hitting the blunt. I was amazed that we all had something in common and it just happened to be weed. When my sisters both admitted to me that they got high, I scolded them because I personally felt that maybe if we smoked together then we wouldn't be at each other's throats so much. They both started laughing, then I started laughing and from there it was like a ripple effect. We all sat in the car and laughed for what seemed like thirty minutes. My dad, who was usually sweet but stiff as a board, seemed to be the coolest person in the world. My sisters were also pretty cool. I was happy but a sadness came over me as well because in my mind I thought about how my sisters and I had spent all this time hating each other when we really could have been having fun and enjoying each other.

After we finished smoking we were all relaxed and ready to tear into some food. Daddy; or should I say; Mr. Cool Man, pulled out a bottle of Visine and passed it around so our eyes wouldn't be red. We stood in the parking lot and clowned him for about fifteen more minutes about that. We then walked to the cafeteria and damn near put them out of business because it seemed as if we ordered everything they had. While we ate, we laughed, talked and reminisced about when we were children. We talked about mom and wondered when she had developed heart problems. We talked about things going on in our lives and for the most part, we became a family. We were no longer estranged from each other or kept secrets from each other. Now I wasn't going to go all out and tell them about my married men but I did let them in on about what was going on with my job and my suspension. They off course all thought that my almost getting raped by a woman was hilarious. They clowned me for the rest of the day until the doctor's came out and told us that the surgery had been successful and we could go in and see mom in groups of two's. I went in with Brandon and had to almost immediately turn back around and come back out. My mom was hooked up to a series of machines and she had tubes in her mouth and nose and IV's in her arms. She looked more like a science project than my mother but I sucked it up because I was just so happy that she was going to be ok.

Mom stayed in Intensive Care for two days before they allowed her to have a normal room. She was in pain and groggy but she was coherent and getting back to her old self. Since my siblings and I were there, my dad went back to work during the day and relieved us in the evenings. Mario was there every day and catered to anything that I needed. Val and her husband came by as did many of our other friends and family members. Jenetta's stanking ass even came by, although I could have done without seeing her. But I did appreciate the gesture because she appeared to be genuinely concerned about my mother. I guess had it been me in the hospital she would have been somewhere celebrating.

The day prior to my mother's release, the doctor came in and talked to me about aftercare. He informed me of certain things that my mother could no longer eat such as foods high in Vitamin K and large amounts of beef due to her having to take a blood thinner that would help her new mechanical heart valves to pump blood correctly. He also informed me that my mom would need help getting around and taking care of herself for at least a month until she was able to do things for herself. When he walked out, I walked out as well. I went outside and sat on bench in the warm sunlight. I looked up at the sky and began to tell God thank you. I sat back and thought about how He had ordered my steps and unbeknownst to me, made it to where I would be able to take care of my mother. It was as if a precious gift had come out of my adversity. My dad had to work and run the businesses, my sisters were married with children and my brother was my brother; careless and irresponsible. I knew that he couldn't properly take care of my mom. I felt so foolish because everything that had happened regarding Candy and my suspension had happened for a reason. God had majestically timed things so that everything fell into place right at the time they were supposed to. I suddenly felt an overwhelming sense of gratitude to God and I couldn't help but to cry out in appreciation and admiration for Him. I think I sat there for an hour just crying and reflecting back on how wonderful and incomparable God is. I finally got myself together, looked to the sky one final time and mouthed "Thank you God" again and headed back upstairs to tend to my mother. As I walked, I thought about how much I missed Him but I just wasn't quite ready to turn from my "wicked ways". He did have my attention though.

Case #32489 Carolyn Who? Carolyn Black

Beep, Beep, Beep. I hit the snooze button for the third time before I got out of bed and headed to the shower. My month long suspension had gone by quicker than I thought it would and I was actually dreading going back to work. For some reason I was nervous because I didn't know what to expect. Mario had been keeping me posted while I was gone and for the most part had informed me that nothing major had changed. He told me that Val hadn't hired anybody new which was a relief to me because I didn't want to have to deal with another female. Hell it was going to be hard enough going back and looking at Jenetta after not having had to deal with her for so long.

As I submerged my body underneath the glorious hot water, my thoughts took me back through all the things I had experienced in the past few months. I just couldn't believe the downward spiral that my life had plummeted into. I thought about my mom, Demarcus, Candy, my cases; everything, even the other men I had been involved with. I had been so wrapped up in taking care of my mom that I hadn't had time to deal with them. My list had dwindled down from four in the beginning to only two now: Brad and Dewayne; both of which I really had no desire to deal with anyway because now that I didn't have Demarcus, the thrill was gone. I didn't have the energy to go out and *find* more men so I made the decision that I was just going to chill out for a while. I was building a new relationship with God and I just didn't have the desire to turn back. In fact I didn't know where I was going or where my life was leading me but in the low state that I was in, I knew it couldn't get any worse.

After being in the shower for what seemed like forever, I got out and began to engage in my daily hygiene ritual. I covered my body with Beautiful lotion, put some Vaseline on my feet and began getting dressed. I put on my accessories and makeup and then I pulled my hair into a side bun. I looked in my full length mirror to make sure that everything was in place and grabbed my brief case and headed out the door. I was worried about leaving my mom but she insisted that she was ok; nevertheless I was still a nervous wreck and was sure that I would be calling her every five minutes to check on her. It was weird going back to work on a Thursday but I was just happy to have a job to go back to.

Upon my arrival back at work, I walked slowly through the front door. Nothing had seemed to change but I on the other hand felt like a totally different person. I felt more humbled because of what I had been through and for the first time in a very long time, I felt afraid. I was afraid that because I was changing, I wouldn't be the same Carolyn anymore. I felt vulnerable again and I didn't know if I would be able to approach my co-workers and/or my cases with the same vigor and confidence that I had in the past. I was tired in my spirit and my vivaciousness was weakened but when I walked into our department and everybody greeted me warmly and welcomed me back to work like I had really been missed, my exuberance became slightly revived .

Val hugged me tightly as I walked into her office. She and I had grown even closer throughout my suspension because she had been there throughout my mother's sickness. But the "welcome back" routine was brief and there was no wasting time in getting back into the swing of things. She immediately handed me a case file regarding some parents who had gotten a report from the doctor's office due to their two year old having unexplainable bruises on his bottom and legs.

I got the address, gathered the necessary documents and traveled to their home to meet with them. When I pulled into the neighborhood, I didn't think I was in the right place because I was used to the majority of my cases being in poor or bad neighborhoods. Not saying that rich people didn't abuse their children, they just did a better job of hiding it. The thought made me reflect back to BaLing and how rich her parents had been and how disgustingly abusive they were to her. We had still been unable to locate her but her baby was safe with his grandparents.

I pulled up to the large and beautiful home and grabbed my papers out to do a quick review. I was thinking to myself, that with names like Josh and Amanda Manor, these people must be white. However, when Josh came to answer the door, I had to pick my mouth up off the ground because before me stood the sexiest, most debonair black man that I had ever encountered in my life with the exception of my father. He looked to be about thirty five years old and he was gorgeous. Dark skinned with piercing dark green/hazel looking eyes, a short fade hair cut, and physique of about 6'4, 215 pounds which was most definitely built Ford tough. But the way he was dressed was what killed me. He had on a white Polo shirt, baggy jeans and a pair of Timberland boots. So I knew right then that although he had some money, he still had some hood swag about himself. I think I stood there so long looking at him that I almost forgot why I was there.

"Umm, hello. You must be Ms. Black. I am Josh Manor." He said as he extended his hand out to shake mine. I was trying my best to keep my composure but at that point and time my panties had started to get wet and I almost forgot that I was there to investigate a CPS report. In my mind I smiled because a piece of the old me was coming back. But I knew that I couldn't regress so I took a deep breath, shook his hand and walked into his house, which was lovely and well decorated. I wanted to compliment him on his nice house and his nice ass but I knew that I had to remain professional because even the beautiful people abused and neglected their children. With that thought in mind I put on my game face and began conducting my investigation.

"So Mr. Manor, you know I'm a child protective services or CPS investigator and my job is to find out what happened that got your family involved with CPS. So do you mind telling me what happened and how your child got the marks and bruises that he sustained?" I asked as sternly and professional as I could.

"Well I actually haven't been here because my job keeps me out of town a lot so you'll probably do better talking to my wife. I'm actually a little pissed about this myself but I don't think that she would hurt our child." He replied.

"Ok, well is your wife home now?" I asked praying that he would say no so I could continue drooling and fantasizing about what I wanted to do to him.

"Well, no but she should be home in about fifteen minutes or so."

"Ok, well Mr. Manor, tell me all that you can about the situation and exactly how long you've been here." I responded politely trying to ignore the fact that my wet panties had began clinging to my Juicy.

He began talking and although I saw his lips moving I had no clue as to what he was saying. All I could think about was him picking me up with those strong, muscular arms and carrying me around the house with my legs wrapped around his face.

"Uh, Ms. Black, are you ok? You have a really strange look on your face."

"Awww damn," I thought to myself. He'd caught me. Shit, I wish I had a Twix so could have something to put in my mouth to give me some time to come up with a clever response.

"I'm sorry Mr. Manor. I've just had a lot going on today and I have to be honest in saying that my mind is really racing right now." I responded hoping that my white woman face wasn't as red as a turnip.

"Oh that's fine Ms. Black. I understand. I actually thought you were thinking about how awesome it would be for you and I to clear everything off this table and see how strong its legs are." I gasped from embarrassment. I was so in shock that I was speechless. And at that point, *I knew* that my white woman face was red as a blazing fire. I didn't realize that my mouth was open until a little bit of slobber ran down the side of my face. I blinked, shook myself back into reality and began clumsily gathering my things. Shit was falling everywhere. I dropped my notebook on the floor, my pens and papers dropped out of my portfolio and I almost fell out of my damn chair trying to pick all the shit up. I was extremely embarrassed but I didn't give a damn cause I knew that I had to get my ass out of there. Now although I loved successful, sexy, *married* black men; I really loved my job and knew that if I didn't get out of there ASAP, I was gonna end up with my legs in the air.

Once I regained my composure I replied, "Mr. Manor, this conversation is very inappropriate and I think that I need to send another investigator to come in and work with your family. Thank you for your time today and someone will be contacting you shortly to discuss your case." And with that being said, I hauled ass getting out of there and didn't even give him time to respond. When I finally did get in my car and onto the highway, I finally started to breath because not only had I made an ass out of myself, I had almost compromised everything I had worked my ass off for, especially since today was only my first day back from suspension.

Once I arrived back at the office, I couldn't wait to go and tell my supervisor, Valerie, what had happened. I knew she would be proud of my professionalism while also getting a good kick out of it. As I was walking in, I ran into Mario and asked him if he'd seen Val. He informed me that she had stepped out for lunch so I walked to my desk and took a deep breath. Once I had gotten myself together, I saw Val walking in but the way she walked in startled me. She was very disheveled and had blood and other stains I couldn't make out all over her clothes. She walked very slowly like she was in a trance. I didn't know if she'd been attacked or what had happened so I jumped up and followed her into her office. I looked around to see if there were a lot of people around and gladly since it was our lunch hour, there were few people there with the exception of Mario who I gave the "Let me handle this" look.

"Val! Girl, what happened?" I asked as I noticed her bloody knuckles and clothes. She sat down in her chair as if she hadn't even heard me and continued to stare at nothing.

"Valerie. Valerie." I said as I gently placed my hand on her shoulder. "Valerie, what happened?" I asked again. She blinked and then looked up at me. In a very low, monotonous voice she replied, "My husband, my husband. He's, he's cheating on me with some woman." She didn't blink, she didn't look at me; she just stared into space.

"Oh my God Valerie, how do you know and why are you so bloody and disheveled?"

"Carolyn, I honestly don't remember anything but going out for a walk for lunch. I really wasn't hungry but it's like God told me to go walk down the street so I did. As I was walking downtown, I noticed my husband's car parked in an alley next to Blue Mesa restaurant. I thought it was weird because you know he works all the way on the east side of the county and he knows that I always pack my lunch so I couldn't figure out why he hadn't called me. So I didn't think anything about it until I walked by and looked into the window and there he was being seated with some woman. Again, I really didn't think anything bad because I know that he has a lot of business associates that he deals with so I figured that it was a business meeting. Then I noticed the way they were sitting. They were in a booth and they sat side by side instead of facing each other. Then I saw the way they were looking at each other." Tears began to stream down her face as she was relived the episode.

"I was so in shock that I still didn't want to believe it. So I watched a little longer and then I saw them kiss and that's the last thing I remember until some large man carried me out of the restaurant and then I started walking back here. All I could think about is, I can't believe this and how long has this been going on and oh my God, my husband is actually cheating on me." I tried to soothe her but I myself was in disbelief because her husband, Maurice seemed to be the perfect husband. We'd all known each other for years and were all good friends. But this confirmed in my mind that there was no way that I was ever going to give myself to a man again because if Maurice would cheat, any man would cheat. I grabbed her some tissues and asked her if she wanted me to take her home. She looked up at me and it's like her whole face changed and she became somebody I didn't know.

"Now why the fuck would I want *you* to take me home of all people. You are a home wreaker just like that whore in the restaurant. Now I see you for who you really are. Matter of fact, get the fuck outta my office." I stood there stunned and hurt at the same time. Was this the same woman who just embraced me with such warmth and love? Was this the same woman who had been by my side throughout my month long suspension? I was in disbelief that she would talk to me like that but I figured it was because she was hurt, angry and emotional. Valerie not only was my supervisor but she was my friend. I wanted to give her some space so I turned to walk out but then the Carolyn Black in me stopped me at the door.

"You know what Val, I know you are hurt and I know you are confused right now, but you don't have no right coming at me like that. Yes I dated married men but I have never dated *your* husband and contrary to popular belief, *us home wreaking whores* don't have affairs by ourselves. Your husband and these other men for the most part pursue us and not the other way around. It takes two to tango boo. Am I justifying what I do? No I'm not, but am I gonna stand here and let you disrespect me because of what Maurice did, HELL NO! Now get your shit so I can take you home cause you done lost your damn mind up in here." She looked at me with fire in her eyes but she knew I was right and she knew I could whoop her ass so she didn't test me. She took a deep breath and gathered her things. I told Mario that we would be leaving for the day and he said that he would cover for me. I gave the Manor case to him and told him that I couldn't take the case due to conflict of interest and he accepted. Since our team didn't work on Fridays I had today and the rest of the weekend to help her get herself together. On our way home she was silent but that was ok because I knew she was trying to come to grips with everything that was going on. I told her that I would help her pack a bag because she was coming to stay with me for the weekend so that she could get herself together and have some space from Maurice.

When we arrived at her house, Maurice's car wasn't there which was a great relief because I knew we wouldn't have any drama. However, when we walked in, the first thing we saw was their poster size wedding picture which hung on the wall in the living room. She immediately lost it and ran to the coat closet, grabbed a baseball bat and began destroying the picture. I didn't try to stop her because I knew that she needed this. I just stood there and watched to make sure that she didn't hurt herself. After she beat the picture to death, she got some of Maurice's clothes and shoes and either tore them to shreds or threw bleach all over them. Exhausted, she plopped down on the couch and sobbed for about thirty minutes. I didn't bother her and instead, I got a broom and dustpan and began cleaning up the mess. She went up to her room and I heard a few more things being destroyed before she reemerged with a suitcase. I laughed in my head because she was always so calm and collected but for one split moment, she'd tapped into her *other* side and I loved it because that's what we all needed to do sometimes in order to stay in touch with reality.

On our way to my house, I stopped by Total Wine and grabbed a couple bottles of Pinot and Mascato. I also called my cousin the weed man and placed an order for a twenty sack of weed. I knew that Maurice smoked marijuana because we, along with some other family and friends had smoked together at one of their family cookouts. But I wasn't sure about Val because I think she was afraid for some of our coworkers to see her smoking as a supervisor. She knew that she could trust me and vice versa so I planned on helping her beam up to Scottie so that she could calm down and relax. When we arrived at my house, I ran her a hot bubble bath and brought her a glass of Moscato. I got the guest room ready for her and found some quick snacks that I could whip up. I knew it was going to be a long night so I rolled a couple blunts and laid everything out in the sun room where I smoked at or went to when I needed to clear my mind from difficult situations.

When she got out of the bath, of course she talked and cried and screamed and I just listened. She also apologized for what she had said earlier and then asked me, "Carolyn, why do men cheat?" Like I was the expert. But in actuality, being the other woman had given me the ability to acquire a lot of knowledge about the issue;

so I just told her what most of the men told me. Dewayne had told me that although he and his wife were both very educated and successful, they lived separate lives. They lived in the same perfect house and attended the perfect parties and functions where they appeared to be the perfect couple when in actuality they barely talked to each other and had very little in common. He told me that I was his friend and lover. He liked me because we could talk and laugh and enjoy each other's company and he didn't have that with his wife. Brad on the other hand was just a cocky butt hole who had an ego the size of the Grand Canyon but at the same time, he'd told me that his wife no longer took pains with herself and had let herself go. He understood that she was a mom now but he also wanted a wife. She paid him little attention and had stopped having sex with him. He told me that he liked me because I was his fantasy and because I was sexy and outgoing and fun. He also liked that I gave him a hard time and didn't take his shit. As far as Demarcus goes, we both laughed about that one. He liked me because I was an around the way girl with some class where as his wife was the hood rat of the year.

"For the most part Val, married men want a wife and they want a fantasy. That's why they cheat. We as women have to figure out how to be both to them, you know like that saying; 'a lady in the streets but a freak in the bed.' And men like women who keep themselves up physically and are fun and sexy. That's just what I've learned. But hell some men are going to cheat regardless, no matter what you do."

"So what category do you think I fall into?" She asked.

"I don't know Val. You have to figure that out for yourself. Hell you may not even fall into a category. I will never understand why Maurice cheated because he seems to be such a loving man. Is there anything that you used to do that you don't do anymore or have you guys stopped talking or what?" She thought for a minute and then as if she had an epiphany she replied, "Carolyn, we haven't had sex in about four or five months."

"Five months!" I exclaimed. "Damn girl! Why? What the hell?"

She dropped her head and replied, "Honestly I really don't do anything anymore and I guess I've just gotten comfortable. I mean, I don't think about being sexy anymore. I'm just a wife I guess."

"So I assume you don't wear lingerie to bed cause you wear those teddy bear jammies you have on now right?" I asked with a giggle. She looked down at her pink and blue PJ's and responded,

"Damn C, I do. I haven't worn anything sexy in a while. But hell, why couldn't he just come talk to me about that if that was the problem? And how is it that this is starting to become my fault. I mean that bastard cheated. Not me." She replied appearing to start getting heated again.

"So he hasn't said anything about it?" I asked. She thought for a minute and then admitted that he had been dropping hints.

"Ok. You know what, go get your shit together and be ready in an hour. We are taking a trip."

"Where we going?" She asked.

"Look Val, if you wanna save your marriage, take my advice and just do as I tell you. You are going to get a makeover." I squealed with excitement because I loved makeovers and as much as I loved Val and she really needed it. She wore grandma clothes and when she didn't have her hair in a grandma hair style; it was in a pony tail. She dressed like an old maid.

She tried to argue with me but I wasn't trying to hear it. I liked Maurice and he wasn't a typical cheater. My experience with married men had taught me a thing or two about what men liked and needed, therefore I was going to give Val a complete transformation which would make her feel sexy without her having to change who she was as a person. So while she was getting her things together, I made a few phone calls, took a quick shower, packed a bag and ushered her out to the car.

We drove to Charlotte, where I took her to meet my stylist, Janice. I made Val give her 1,000 dollars, which I knew Val had because she was very frugal and saved every penny she didn't spend on bills. She never wanted to shop and rarely did things for herself unless it was a necessity. I trusted Janice because I knew that she could look at Val's style and simply jazz it up. After giving Janice the money, I took Val to my favorite beauty salon so that she could get her hair, nails and feet done. We also got facials and drank wine. Of course I indulged myself as well because I mean hey, I didn't want her to go through this alone after all.

After hair and nails, we went to the mall to Victoria's Secret to get lingerie. I could tell that she felt better about herself already by the way she smiled and swung her hair as she walked. Each time we walked past a mirror I caught her admiring herself which made me laugh. Her pretty chocolate skin was glowing and her shoulder length black hair fell around her face. The only thing left was to let Janice put the finishing touches on her wardrobe because she had a cute shape which was always hidden underneath oversized grandma slacks and blouses and chunk heeled shoes from 1995. The horrendous outfit she was currently wearing was composed of some straight legged, faded out blue jeans, big flowered flip flops and a bright orange tank top. And this wasn't an "I'm depressed and don't feel like getting dressed up" outfit either. This was her typical way of dressing.

After I helped her pick out some lingerie and various pajama sets, we left the mall and headed to the Marriot Hotel where I had a friend who gave me a major discount on a hotel room for the weekend. On the way there we talked about sex and I was very inquisitive about her sex life.

"So Val, let's get down to the nitty gritty. Do you give head?" Taken aback, she looked at me as if I'd just eaten a pile of shit and was spitting it back in her face.

"Hell no I don't do that nasty shit. That's gross." She replied, looking repulsed.

"Awwwww hell Val. You don't give your husband head? I mean that's a given. I don't give my men head because their wives should be doing that but damn my husband would get slurped up. Girl you betta get with the program. Please believe what you won't do, another woman will." I shook my head and laughed, "Damn Val, this is gonna be a long weekend." She looked at me like a deer caught in headlights. I assured her that I wasn't going to make her do anything but I did plan on getting a banana and showing her how to give some good head.

We arrived at the hotel, checked in and headed to our room. Janice came shortly after with a shit load of clothes, shoes and accessories. She showed Val how to put the outfits together from the top to bottom. I loved Janice because by the time she got done with Val, she looked like a straight diva. Val of course liked what she saw and I could see her self confidence increasing. By the time Janice was done, we were both pooped and decided to chill in the room for the night. The next day, we slept in, ordered room services and watched movies. She checked her phone and found that she had like ten messages, mostly all from Maurice and one from her mother who she called back. Her mom informed her that Maurice had called her and told her everything. When Val hung up the phone from talking to her mother, she was laughing. I personally thought she was crazy until she told me what she was laughing about. Apparently she'd damn near killed Maurice and the woman while also practically destroying the restaurant. By the end of the story we were both laughing so hard that our stomachs were hurting. Around 9:00 that night, I announced that we were going out on the town for the night. She accepted, but reluctantly.

So we both got dressed and prepared to head out. Janice had gotten Val a fitted silver dress that came above her knees and had a drastic drop in the back that stopped right above the crack of her ass; revealing her entire backside. Janice had put the accessories and shoes with each outfit for Val because she had also realized how fashionably challenged Val was. I did her makeup for her and by the time I was done, I was almost jealous because I was used to being the center of attention. She looked absolutely gorgeous. Her dress fit her like a glove and her smile was so radiant that no one would have known that she was recovering from a cheating husband.

When we arrived at the club, we went straight to the bar and started drinking. I kept it cool because I wanted Val to be able to let loose therefore I only had a few drinks. The music was jumping and we danced until our legs hurt. Although it was a dirty thirty club, they still played the new music and some of the hits from our younger days like the Three Six Mafia, Little Jon and the East Side boys and the Cash Money Millionaires. As we went to the bar to grab another drink, we ran into Mario and one of his friends.

"Hey Mario, what you doing here?" We asked as we both hugged him. "Dag, is this dude stalking me?" I thought to myself.

"Shit, I had to get away for awhile. I've had a hell of a week at work so me and my homeboy decided to come down here and see what was popping. Apparently no matter how hard I try to get away from work, it just seems to follow me." He said with a giggle. "What are y'all doing here?" He asked.

"Same thing." I replied.

"Val, don't take this the wrong way but you look beautiful. I ain't never seen you look like this before." Mario said to Val.

"Thanks. This is the *new* Val baby." She said a little louder than necessary.

"Well, *new* Val and Carolyn, this is my homeboy Trey."

"Hey, nice to meet you." We both replied as we shook Trey's hand.

"Let us buy y'all a drink."

"Well go right ahead. I ain't turning down no free drinks." Val slurred, not really needing to drink anything else. Mario looked at me and gave me a "what the heck is going on here?" look. I giggled and simply shrugged my shoulders. After we got our drinks, we all toasted and took a shot of vodka. Trey asked Val to dance and in her drunken state, she readily went, leaving me at the bar with Mario. In my buzzed state I noticed that he looked and smelled really good and I loved a man who smelled good.

Taking me out of my trance, he said, "Ok Carolyn spill it. What's really going on? You know I saw Val when she came back to the office Thursday looking like a serial killer. Now she looking like a Hollywood star. What's up with that?"

"That ain't my business to tell." I replied.

"Bullshit. I saw Maurice at the hospital Thursday afternoon. I had to go check on one of my kids and on my way in I saw him and some broad coming out all scratched up and bandaged up. The woman had a black eye and Maurice had stitches in his head." I busted out laughing because in my head I saw Val putting a hurting on Maurice and the woman although I didn't even know what she looked like. I guess Val wasn't so innocent after all.

"What did Maurice say happened?" I asked.

"All he said was that Val jumped on him. He didn't go into details. But the funny thing about it is that he looked like he was turned on by the fact that she'd jumped on him and that poor woman he was with was all messed up. So I assume that he must have got caught cheating or something. I didn't wanna think that because you know Maurice is my boy and I don't see him cheating. But when I put two and two together and see Val down here with her "hot girl" dress on, I guess my assumption is right."

I shook my head and laughed; refusing to spill the beans. He asked me to dance so we went and finished the night out on the dance floor. When the party was over we found that our hotels were within the same vicinity, so he helped me walk and an overly drunk Val to the cab. His homeboy had a late night booty call so he left. When we got back to the hotel we took Val to the room and I told him I would come holler at him once I got Val in her pajamas and into bed. I made her take some aspirin before I let her go to sleep. Then I put the trash can beside the bed and rolled her over on her side. I then put on some shorts and a tee shirt and headed to Mario's hotel. When I walked in, he was rolling a blunt and I immediately got excited.

"Mario, I didn't know you smoked. Hell yea! Where we gonna go spark at?"

"We can go to my car." He responded as he sealed the blunt with a lick of his saliva. And that's exactly what we did. We smoked and talked and laughed about Val and Maurice. It was so cool being with him because I could just relax and be myself. I wasn't concerned about my appearance or if I my breath was super fresh. I was simply having a good time. I knew Mario had a crush on me but I hadn't been interested in any man that wasn't married or rich because I had long given up on the monogamous kind of relationships. And although Mario was very handsome with caramel skin and really pretty white teeth, he was out of the question for me.

After we finished smoking, we checked in on Val who was passed out and snoring. I then went back to Mario's room because he had pizza and chips and to a high person, that was the answer to a prayer. We ate, talked and listened to the radio. I really liked Mario and I was really enjoying myself until he started getting too serious.

"So Carolyn, why ain't you married?"

"Because Mario, you see what happens to people when they get married. Who would have thought that Maurice of all people would cheat?"

"Yea but, all men don't cheat and I personally feel like Maurice got caught up. I mean, I ain't trying to be funny but Val had it coming because she just didn't appeal to the eye. She's pretty but not sexy and men like a sexy woman. The woman I saw Maurice with was very attractive and not because she was exceptionally pretty but more because of the way she carried herself. "

"Ok so you are justifying what Maurice did?" I asked knowing from being the other woman that he was right, but I just wanted to play devil's advocate.

"No not at all. He was wrong but I honestly don't think that Val didn't play a part in it. But I'm not talking about them, I'm talking about you. Now I don't know if it's the weed and liquor that's talking right now but I have to say this."

He paused, took a deep breath and said, "Fuck it. I'm just going to say it. Listen Carolyn, I have liked you since the first day I saw you in grad school. You were wearing a pink sweat shirt, black tights and UGGs. You had your hair in a pony tail and you didn't have any makeup on except lip gloss. And I remembered thinking that you were the most beautiful woman I'd ever seen in my life. I was so intimidated by you until I got to know you." He stopped long enough to give me a sheepish look and make sure that I was listening and then he continued.

"Look, I know I may not be the type of guy that you

usually go for but I just want to show you something different." He paused again and slowly shook his head with confidence as he began softly declaring to me and himself, "I'm a good man Carolyn, I'm a good man...and I ain't never felt this way about a woman before.....you should give me a try." He rubbed his hands together nervously as he waited for me to respond which at that time I was incapable of doing.

My body felt hot and flushed. I wasn't surprised by his declaration because I'd always known how he felt about me. But nevertheless, I wasn't expecting him to actually say it out loud. I started feeling uncomfortable and for the second time this week, I wished I had a Twix. Being that I didn't have a Twix, I opted to take an extended gulp of soda in order to stall. The scary thing was that I may have been feeling the same way all along but because of all the distractions I had, I just didn't see it. I began thinking back to how he'd always been there for me no matter what was going on, especially when I was dealing with my mother. I also thought about how we'd laugh and joke or how I always made it a point to end up sitting near him no matter where we were or what we were doing. And one major thing that really stuck out amongst the rest was that when I was with Mario I was always smiling and I felt safe. I started to realize that although I'd been fighting it, I really had strong feelings for Mario. But I didn't know if it was because I had no obligations to him or now strong desire to go out of my way to impress him? Or were these feelings that I was feeling at this moment the result of an opportunity to rebound from what I been through; a means of getting over my hurt? What if I was just emotional, what if I was just tripping, and what if it was the liquor and the weed clouding my judgment? What if? What if? What if....what if was real this time? He made me feel comfortable, therefore allowing me to be myself. I could burp and curse and be lackadaisical around him. There was no need to go overboard in trying to please him because he was pleased with me just being me.

As I began to have this revelation about the possibility that I really liked Mario, my palms began to sweat because I was so confused. If I had had these feelings all along, why hadn't I realized it sooner? I didn't want to say anything that was out of context so I licked my lips and looked down at the table. I needed time to gather my thoughts because I wasn't prepared for the emotional response that was going on inside my body. I hadn't felt this way about a man...ever; even Demarcus. I'd realized during my healing process that my feelings for Demarcus were superficial and based off a lie that I'd kept telling myself over and over again. Mario had started out being my friend which was something that I'd never had with any other man. I didn't have the codependent feelings that I felt for Demarcus because these feelings that I felt were pure, raw and innocent. When Mario did things for me, he never asked for anything in return and he never made me feel like he was doing things out of false modesty to get my attention. He was genuine and that was also something that I'd never felt before.

I was beginning to feel scared and my heart began beating really fast. What was going on? Why was this happening now? What would he think about me if he really knew me? And with that thought, I began to fear that I had all these questions running through my mind because for once in my life, I'd come across a man who I felt that I wasn't good enough for. He deserved a pure woman who wasn't battered and broken; a woman who could give him 100 percent. Not a woman who could only give him fragments of her heart. Maybe that was the reason why I'd ignored or overlooked any feelings or possibilities that presented themselves in regards to a relationship with Mario. I now understood that I really had wanted him but because of the Scarlet Letter I bore on my chest, I didn't want to subject him to my world of madness.

Realizing that I'd gone into deep thought for an overly extended amount of time, he broke my train of thought. "Carolyn, for God's sake say something. You've been sitting there looking at the table for what seems like forever. Talk to me; tell me what you're thinking. I know that we are both a little intoxicated but my feelings are real no matter what state of mind I'm in."

Opting to take the cop out method, I finally began to speak. "Boy bye, go on somewhere with that. Let's watch a movie."

He cut me off and replied, "Carolyn, that's bullshit. Stop

trying to change the subject and answer me." My palms began to sweat excessively as I squirmed around in my seat trying to conjure up another excuse.

"Listen Mario, we have been friends for so long, there is no way that we could make it into anything else. It would just ruin our relationship plus we work together and I mean; it just wouldn't work."

"Carolyn, you're still bullshitting me. Come on now. Tell me how you feel." He responded.

Starting to get defensive and trying to take the heat off myself, I stood up and almost yelled out, "Look, I don't think I could reciprocate the feelings that you have for me. I don't feel the same way."

Still not buying it, he redirected the conversation back to where it had started. "Carolyn if you're scared say you're scared but don't give me some bullshit ass excuse. Keep it real. This is me you talking to and we've never kept it anything but real with each other. I will still be your friend regardless but at least I let you know how I feel."

I didn't like having my "keeping it real" card pulled because I prided myself on speaking my mind and telling people how I felt but this was different because I was having to expose my vulnerabilities. And this new vulnerability crap was starting to get on my nerves but I elected to go ahead and tell the truth so I put it out there to him.

"Well since you put it like that, ok. I'm scared. I like you too Mario. A lot. But I just realized it and I really don't understand it. Plus you don't know me like you think you do. I know this is the same old soap box that everybody jumps on but yes I've been hurt a lot and here lately I've taken on a different perspective when it comes to dating and relationships. Some of the things I've done may not seem acceptable to you but it is what it is and that's the life I've chosen to live. I'm not the woman that you deserve Mario. I'm not pure and wholesome. I'm broken Mario. I've been perverted and tainted." I said candidly while trying to hold back my tears. He looked at me and smiled. Then he shook his head as he let out a giggle which made me want to sock him right in the eye because I felt like he was mocking me.

"Carolyn, I know more than you think and I don't care about that. If I liked you because you were perfect then I wouldn't be here. I like you because you're confident, you're strong and you're a good person. I know the real you, not the one who tries to be tough and put on a front like she doesn't have any feelings." He gently pulled me by my arm and pulled me down to where the side of his face was against my ear.

"Let me mend your broken heart." He whispered. He turned my face to his face. We were so close that I could feel his breath brushing against my skin. He looked in my eyes and didn't blink as he leaned in and kissed me. I resisted and pulled away because I was too confused to go further. I didn't want to be a bad girl with him because I wanted to be pure for once in my life. Plus the thought of my pizza, weed and liquor breath now mattered to me.

"Damnit!" I thought to myself. Now I'd have to start paying attention to stuff like that. "Damn, you Mario!" I wanted to scream.

Noticing my discomfort, he pulled back. "Am I moving too fast Carolyn?" He asked.

I began to cry, which made me angry. Over this past month I'd become a big bucket of tears and I was beginning to loathe it. I wanted my tough, emotionless self back. These feelings were to raw for me and it made me feel weak.

"Carolyn, you don't have to be afraid of me. I won't hurt you." He whispered as he held my hand. I blushed. I wanted to let go but I was paralyzed by fear and doubt. I couldn't believe it. I actually encountered a man who was making me, Carolyn Black, feel intimidated. Just then, the radio started playing, "Have You Ever Loved Somebody" by Freddie Jackson. He got up out of his seat and held his hand out to me.

"Will you dance with me?" He asked. I blushed again and coyly accepted his hand. He put his hand on the small of my back and led me to the middle of the floor. He wrapped his arms around me and I melted because being in his arms felt so good. I let my guard down, exhaled and laid my head on his shoulder. As we swayed to the music, he rubbed my hair and gently entwined his fingers within mine. My body heat began to rise and at that moment I wanted him badly. I wanted to take things slowly with him but the old Carolyn began to rise like the Phoenix. I grabbed his face and began kissing him forcefully. But he pulled back and wrapped his arms around my waist, gently positioned my head on his shoulder and resumed dancing slowly to the beat of the music. I was super embarrassed but more than anything I felt raw. The old Carolyn retreated back to where she'd been hiding and let the new and I must say, emotional Carolyn take back over. Mario began to caress my hair along with my ego. He made me feel comfortable like he always had and then I realized that I didn't want it to be like it had with all the other men where I tried to control everything. For once, I wanted to be submissive and allow him to take the lead. And as if he'd read my mind, he kissed me so sweetly that tears began to roll down my face. "Damn you emotional Carolyn!" I thought to myself. Then the thoughts of my breath came back to my mind and I quickly turned my head.

"Um, my breath is probably terrible." I said meekly. He burst into laughter and said, "Um, I've been eating and drinking *and* smoking the same things you have so if you can deal with mine then I can definitely deal with yours." Beginning to feel comfortable again, I replied, "Well mine must smell like shit because yours is howling." We both shared a laugh and he tightened his grip. He kissed me and I returned his kiss. We continued to kiss and dance until both our bodies were so overcome with desire that neither of us could deny the inevitable. He took my hand and led me to the bed. He began slowly undressing me and I, him. Once we were both naked, I looked at his rock solid body. He was chiseled like a sculpture and had very fine straight hairs on his chest. He also had several tattoos, which I loved.

A chill ran down my back because I was so afraid of crossing the friend to lover line. I knew that if we made love then there was no turning back. Sensing my reluctance he asked, "Are you sure you want to do this? We can just lay here if you want to." I took a deep breath and whispered, "No, its ok." He smiled and gently laid me on the bed. He kissed me softly and to lighten the mood and calm me down, he said, "Now look, after I get through putting this thang on you, don't be stalking me o.k.?" I busted out laughing and wanted him even more because in my heart I knew he was different from all the others.

He removed my clothes. He kissed me, he touched me and he...ate me. And the way he licked my Juicy was out of this world. He teased her, he sucked her and he cherished her. I had to put the pillow over my face to keep the patrons in the adjoining rooms from hearing me scream. I grabbed onto my breasts and squeezed them in order to diverge some of the overwhelming sensation from my Juicy. After his mouth had had its way with my Juicy, he filled her up with his Johnson that was not too big, nor to small but it was just right. He touched me all over as we fell into a harmonious rhythm with each other. He sucked my breasts and tantalized my nipples. I came, and I came hard. It was exhilarating.

"You ok?" He whispered in my ear, not missing a beat.

"Yes." I hissed. "But if it's ok with you, I would like to return the favor."

"Ms. Black you can do whatever you want to do to me." He replied. And with that being said, I rolled him over without missing a beat and began riding him. Being on top made me feel liberated. I didn't feel controlling per say, I was simply *enjoying* myself; while also enjoying the way I was driving him crazy. Sweat glistened on my body and my hardened nipples stood erect. He grabbed my hips and squeezed them as he prepared to cum. Realizing that in our sex crazed desire for each other we had not put on a condom; he quickly lifted me off him and came on the floor. Once he had completely released, he laid back on the bed and pulled me close to him. He put his arm around me and we were both silent. I didn't know what he was thinking but once the afterglow had worn off; along with the weed and alcohol, my fear and insecurities began to return.

"You ok?" He asked.

"Yeah, I'm fine. You?" I replied, telling a little white lie.

"I'm beyond fine. I told you I was gonna put that thang on

you girl." He said, mimicking the voice of a dirty old man. I couldn't help but to laugh. He kissed the top of my forehead, got up and retrieved our drinks and the remaining portion of the blunt we'd been smoking earlier. We smoked, talked and made love again. But once he fell asleep, I quickly got dressed and returned to my room. Val was in the same position I'd left her in and she was snoring loud enough to shake the walls. Once I showered and finally laid down, I began to cry because I felt like a whore. Although I had these strong emotions for Mario, I hadn't made him pursue me and I'd given him my body too easily; without any definite boundaries or set guidelines. Just as I had done in the past with the men I'd dealt with prior to my involvement with married men. Old Carolyn scolded me for my stupidity but she reassured me that she would protect me and never allow anything like that to happen again…

Want to know what happens next with Carolyn Black?

Stay tuned for
Social Work: The Carolyn Black Chronicles
Part II

BIOGRAPHY OF LARONYA NICOLE TEAGUE

Laronya Teague is an aspiring writer who currently works as a Family Preservation Therapist. She is a graduate of Winston-Salem State University where she obtained her Bachelor's Degree in Psychology and NC A&T State University where she graduated with a Master's Degree in Agency Counseling. *SOCIAL WORK: THE CAROLYN BLACK CHRONICLES* is her first published novel. She is currently working on the sequel: *SOCIAL WORK: THE CAROLYLN BLACK CHRONICLES PART II.*

Made in the USA
Middletown, DE
21 July 2015